Early praise for Marjoram & Mace

"delivers a satisfying quota of twists and turns...a rewarding, unstoppable read."
—Ann Vanderhoof, author of *An Embarrassment of Mangoes* and *The Spice Necklace*

"Fast and fun – a one-sitting read that will leave you hoping to meet Detective Segal again."
—Beth Leonard, author of *The Voyager's Handbook*

"romps along. I got hooked and read until early in the morning."
—Lin Pardey, author of *Self-Sufficient Sailor*

"a different kind of whodunnit, one that entertains as much as it pleases. Few authors could have dunnit as well as this."
—John Vigor, author of *The Seaworthy Offshore Sailboat*

MARJORAM & MACE

Nonfiction by Don Casey

This Old Boat

Sensible Cruising: The Thoreau Approach

Dragged Aboard: A Cruising Guide for the Reluctant Mate

Don Casey's Complete Illustrated Sailboat Maintenance Manual

100 Fast & Easy Boat Improvements

Sailboat Hull & Deck Repair

Inspecting the Aging Sailboat

Sailboat Electrics Simplified

Canvaswork & Sail Repair

Sailboat Refinishing

MARJORAM & MACE

DON CASEY

Stick Pony

M · I · A · M · I

This is a work of fiction.
Names, characters, places, and incidents
are the product of the author's imagination or
are used fictitiously. Any resemblance to actual persons,
living or dead, businesses, companies, events, or
locales is entirely coincidental.

STICK PONY PRESS
MIAMI

ISBN   979-8-9891955-1-0

Library of Congress Control Number: 2023947611

*Typeset in Palatino Linotype,
originally designed by Hermann Zapf in 1951.
Book cover and design: Steve Manley, Overleaf Design Ltd.*

For Olga
the sun, the moon
and the
North Star

There are times in life
when people must know
when not to let go. Balloons
are designed to teach
small children this.

—Terry Pratchett, *A Hat Full of Sky*

MARJORAM & MACE

1987

FRIDAY, LATE AFTERNOON

HE FISH HAD MADE A REAL MESS OF HER. The nibbling had started at the softer fleshy areas of her face, breasts, and thighs, leaving them pocked.

I looked up from the body and out across the water, my eyes following the span of the bridge across Card Sound to the banks on the other side – Monroe County. If this was a homicide, any clues the body might have provided about who killed her had been washed away. And with no crime scene either, I found myself wishing the tide had been ebbing instead of flooding when she surfaced so she would have grounded over there.

"Well, there's Detective Segal. You sure took your time."

I turned to see Horace Graves walking on the firm bank of dead coral, out from under the shadow of the bridge, grinning from ear to ear.

"Don't give me any crap, FB, you know this is the wrong time of day to be driving all the way down here. And on a Friday, drawing a floater ahead of the weekend."

Horace and I had been partners more than, Jesus, 20 years back. Fresh out of the academy, we had tooled around with big guns on our hips, a 12-gauge clipped to the dash, confident that we were throwing the fear of God into every crook and hustler who saw us in our crisp, brown uniforms. It wasn't pleasant to recall what a gung-ho type I had been.

"And why are you here?"

"The fisherman who spotted her called it in from the Monroe side. One of our guys responded, called your people, I came down just to have a look, been guarding the scene till a detective from Dade finally showed up. 'Course, I figured it might be you." Horace turned to the body, shaking his head. "Glad she's not mine."

"Well, on the bright side, her killer got unlucky."

Horace looked at me and flashed his trademark grin. "Uh-huh. How you been, Stick?" Horace has a weight problem. So do I, for that matter, but in the opposite direction. When we cruised together, we were known as Fat Boy and Stick.

"Not bad," I said, returning my focus to the body. The skin of her hands and feet had swollen in the seawater and separated from the underlying flesh so that she appeared to be wearing pale, wrinkled, oversized latex gloves and shoes, but with shiny red toenails and fingernails popping out of the ends.

I looked up at Marjorie Foster, the senior scene investigator from the medical examiner's office who had arrived before me and was holding up the sheet covering the body. "Hey, Madge. Any guess at how long she's been in the water?"

"Three, four days tops?" She scrunched her face to emphasize her uncertainty. "Given water temps this time of year and assuming she was not dead too long before she went in, that's what we're looking at for her to come back up and bring that cinderblock with her."

As I pulled examination gloves out of my pocket, I felt the

familiar mix of revulsion and affront. No matter how many times I see what is left of a person after life has been blasted out of them, beat out of them, cut out of them, or has just oozed out of them, that mix of feelings is always there. It's no different than what most people would feel, but a cop's job is to tilt the scale – to enforce civility, not just mourn its loss. The day I feel just revulsion, I will turn in the badge.

"I can tell you this," Marjorie Foster continued. "She surfaced near here. Her back is clean, very few predation marks. She'd have been floating face down, at least the upper part of her back, her shoulders, exposed, and if she'd been drifting for even an hour, the birds would have done a number on that part of her, doesn't take long."

"Thanks, Madge."

Jane Doe's hair was mostly dry now, on the red end of the blonde spectrum. I guessed her height at around five feet four inches, but the body was so bloated that I thought that estimate might be way off. She wore only a bikini bottom, a blue floral print, the flowers all stretched out of shape. I knelt to look inside the suit for a size, but I couldn't get even a finger under the band. I asked Foster's assistant to cut the bottom off for me and I showed him where I wanted the cuts.

I looked at the concrete block her feet were bound to. Every house and apartment building in South Florida has been built with blocks just like it for the past 50 years. It looked new, except a corner was broken off. I figured I might find out who made it but finding out who bought it would be impossible.

The cord that attached Jane Doe to the block was no more distinctive. It was ordinary packaging string, the brown, fuzzy kind – jute, I think it's called. I had some at home that I got at Eckerd or Woolworth, someplace like that.

"Size five." Horace was looking at the cut bathing suit Foster's assistant had handed him. "This was a small lady a couple of days ago. Label says Connie Banko; she didn't get it at Kmart."

"Who pulled her out? The fisherman?"

Horace shook his head. "Says he didn't touch her. Trooper got here first. Name's Watson. He went in after her, from this shore." Horace nodded down at the bank we all stood on.

"No jewelry?"

"Nothing. Just like you see her." Horace pointed. "That's Watson. You want to talk with him?"

I shook my head. "Later." I looked over at the forensic photographer. "Hey Charlie. You about finished taking pictures?"

"Yeah, unless you want special shots. I've got another call up in Biscayne Gardens."

"If you didn't already, take a couple of close shots of this before you go." I was still squatting at her feet and I indicated the string around her ankles. "FB, look at this." The jute cord was wrapped around each ankle and through the holes in the block, around and around, like a Roman sandal. One ankle was attached to one side of the block, the other to the other side. It was the neatness that struck me; the cord never crossed itself, each loop lying flat against the next.

After Charlie had taken four additional shots of her feet, I wished him luck with the traffic, then I turned back to Madge Foster. "Cut her free of the block and you can have her. I'll take the cord and the block. When do you think you might have an accurate PMI?" PMI was short for post-mortem interval – how much time has passed between death and the body's discovery. "She's in decent shape. I'll try and get you preliminary cause and time by late Sunday or Monday. Tox report will be days later unless you put a rush on it; they're way backed up with OD's."

While they zipped Jane Doe into a bag and took her away, I went to talk briefly with the fisherman, mostly out of politeness. People who discover bodies want to at least be asked about it by the investigating officer. You can't blame them, but it's usually a waste of time. Anyway, he did report it and waited around, so that ought to be worth something.

I also talked with the trooper to make sure Horace had relayed everything. He too had nothing to add beyond grousing about his wet socks.

I put the block, the cord, and the bagged bikini bottom in the trunk of my car and then walked Horace back to his. He tried again to get me to quit Metro and come down to the Keys. "Paycheck might be smaller, but you've got a better chance of making it to retirement."

"Somebody's got to go after the bad guys," I said.

"Doesn't have to be you." Horace said, climbing into his car.

"Maybe not." But it did have to be me. I knew it and so did Horace. "See ya, Fat Boy."

Horace smiled. "You take care, Stick," he said, then gunned his cruiser in a spray of gravel back toward Key Largo.

I spent about an hour walking the bridge, across on one side, back across on the other, searching for some sign of where she might have gone over, but I didn't find any. She could have been dropped into the water from a boat, I supposed, but then it wouldn't make sense to drop her near a bridge, too many better places if you had a boat. If you didn't have a boat, the remote Card Sound Bridge spanning a deep channel was perfect. It was 13 pitch-black miles from any main road, with little to no traffic after the nearby Alabama Jacks roadhouse closed at dusk. I was sure she had come off this bridge.

2

MONDAY, MORNING

"MARY FRANCES CLARKE. BEEN MISSING since Tuesday, almost a week. Didn't pick her kids up from school. Husband reported it."

The squad room on Monday morning was a wall of sounds from ringing phones, shouting mouths, and clacking typewriters. I stopped pressing keys on my own Selectric and looked at the missing-person file Emilio Sanchez dropped on my desk.

He continued, "Your floater from Friday matched the description, so I got her dental records. The ME says no question, she ain't missing anymore."

I picked up the file. "Anything in this, Sanch?"

He shook his head. "She lives – she lived – down off Old Cutler. Well off. Husband runs some kind of investment company or something. She was home at one-thirty when the pool service came by. Supposed to pick up her two kids from school at three, never showed, school called the father about three-forty. He picked up the kids…" Sanch paused and glanced quickly in the file, "at about four twenty-five. Just before six, he called it in, from home."

"Does he know?"

"That she's dead? Not unless he did it."

I raised an eyebrow. Sanch shook his head and continued. 'I got no reason to suspect this guy. He's been helpful, seems as

7

concerned as any husband with a missing wife."

"ME have any more? Rape? Drugs?"

"She said maybe tomorrow."

I wasn't surprised.

"This a homicide?"

"She was attached to a cinderblock."

Sanch nodded. "Her car was there, and her purse. The husband said the front door was locked, the rear not. Nothing unusual inside, no signs of a struggle, nothing missing."

"Except," I glanced down at the file again, "Mary Frances Clarke."

"Right." Sanch shook his head, "Broad daylight...poof."

When Sanch left, I read the thin file and said the victim's name aloud a couple of times, repeated it in my head. I didn't know Mary Clarke, never would, but she and I were now connected. I'd be saying her name over and over in the coming days and I didn't want to have to glance down at my notes when talking to a grieving family member or friend. Mary Frances Clarke.

Next, I called Roberts & Wilson, Pension Consultants, to find out if Mr. Roger Clarke was at work or at home. He was at work, so I turned off my typewriter, picked up my jacket, and went down to the garage.

*   *   *

Roberts & Wilson was at 840 Biltmore Way. That turned out to be a new high-rise office building just to the west of Miracle Mile. I parked in front and rode the elevator up to the 12th floor. When the elevator doors opened, I faced an imposing pair of oak doors that stood at least 10 feet tall. Since these were the only doors but for the stairway, the restrooms, and a narrow door I took to be a storage closet, I surmised that the company occupied the whole floor.

When the receptionist called, Roger Clarke came out immediately to greet me. I introduced myself as Detective Frank Segal from the Metro-Dade police department. Mr. Clarke was a good three inches taller than me and his impeccably tailored suit made me feel a bit shabby. He had a square face with flat surfaces and sharp angles. Brown hair graying at the temples. Brown eyes, but of an unusually light shade made more noticeable by the dark circles around them. Mr. Clarke had not been sleeping well, and despite the neat hair and crisp suit, he looked worn. Those troubled eyes told me he had guessed why I was there.

He led me back to an office that was about the same size as mine, except that I share mine with 17 other cops. As we entered, I was still deciding how best to play it. There's no good way to tell someone we've found his wife's body.

"She's...she's dead?" He had closed the door and was leaning against it, his right hand still holding on to the knob.

"Let's sit down, Mr. Clarke." He was big and broad-shouldered, but that didn't mean what I was about to confirm wouldn't flatten him. I had still been in uniform when the wife of a lineman with the Dolphins had been killed in a car accident and I was the one to tell him. He was huge but he gave a little whimper and went down like an imploded building. I did not want the two-hundred-plus pounds of Mr. Clarke lying on the floor against the door.

There was a seating area near the door. Roger Clarke released his grip on the doorknob and stepped over to a nice sofa. I took one of the facing chairs. He looked straight at me and waited.

"I'm sorry." I intended to say more, but he began to cry, restrained at first, then giving in with his entire body. It was my turn to wait.

There was nothing about his grief that didn't seem real. Had I not been around long enough to close the cases of a dozen grief-stricken husbands who'd killed their wives, it would be hard for me to imagine the man before me as a murderer, but I was jaded, skeptical of displays of grief. I couldn't decide if the job had made me more perceptive or just less human.

I wanted to feel sorry for him, a man in obvious pain, but I couldn't. I was still affronted by the sight of a dead woman on the shoreline. This sobbing company president could be her killer. The courts considered him innocent until proven guilty, but I didn't. Until I knew better, my presumption was guilt.

Roger Clarke regained his composure, but he kept his head down for a couple of minutes. I didn't think he was much beyond 40, but his hair was thinning on top. When he looked up, his eyes were painfully red.

"How? What happened?" His speech was strained.

"I don't have the report back from the medical examiner yet. I'll know more then." I spoke in an even, measured tone, matter of fact.

"What happened?" he repeated. "Where did you find her?"

I told him the what and the where, leaving out details I didn't want to share. Yet, despite the bare story I told, I could see reflected in his eyes the horror of his wife standing upright on the bottom of Card Sound, her feet attached to a concrete block. If he was acting, he was good. Then, his mind rejected the idea completely.

"No, wait. You've got the wrong person. It has to be a mistake. There's no…a, a fucking block? That's Mafia shit. Mary's a housewife, a mother with two…" He paused, "No. Mary's still missing. That's not who you found."

"We have her dental records," I said, "the medical examiner made a positive identification."

"I don't care. Mary's teeth are like a million others. Or you got the wrong records. Jesus, you guys have fucked this up."

When I decided to bring along the evidence bag containing the bikini bottom I hadn't known why, but I knew now. I couldn't let him convince himself that we'd not found his wife, his wife's body. I pulled the bag from my jacket pocket and laid it on top of the crisp Wall Street Journal on the low table between us. He reached out for it, then just let his fingers drift above the clear plastic, tracing the outline of one of the flowers. He again began to cry.

It didn't last long this time. Then he stood and went across the office to an inconspicuous door near his desk, opened it, and disappeared. I heard the muted sound of running water and he was soon back, looking more composed, but beaten down. I had put the bagged bikini bottom back inside my jacket.

"Wh…" He cleared his throat, "Why?"

"I don't know yet. When I find out who, I'll learn why."

"Was she…raped?" He was still trying to fit this into a world he could understand.

I did not have a report from the ME yet, but I saw no reason to add that to the horror I had already handed him, so I shook my head and said, "As of now we have no reason to believe she was sexually assaulted."

"Then why?" he asked, but before I could answer he added, "Can you find who?"

I said I would try. I gave him a card with a number on it and told him how to make the necessary arrangements to claim his wife's body. I told him that I wanted to look at his house, her house, and we set that up for the following afternoon. I stood and told him that I was sorry. I tried to feel it as I said it because I wanted to.

He led me out of his office and as we passed his secretary's desk, they exchanged a look. She suddenly appeared stricken. It was the kind of non-verbal communication that is only possible between people who know each other well, very well.

I had not seen her when we came in, so she must not have been at her desk. I tried to take her all in now. She was Latin and quite beautiful, although neither of those are particularly distinguishing features in a county swamped with beautiful Latin women. Late twenties, dark hair, a lot of it, and an olive complexion. Her troubled eyes were almost black. She wore red, a stand-up collar giving a regal note to her appearance. The brass plate on her desk read CARMEN DEL PORTILLO.

Roger Clarke left me at the reception area. I headed toward the entry doors, then slowed and made a show of slapping my pockets. "My notebook," I said aloud. When I turned, Roger Clarke was gone. I walked back down the corridor to find Miss del Portillo's desk empty and Clarke's office door closed.

Back at the receptionist, I held up my pad and flashed a bright smile. "They found it. Miss del Portillo seems nice, but I don't remember her from last time."

"She is nice," she agreed. "She's only been here about, maybe, three months."

3

TUESDAY, MORNING

"Segal, i got the final pmi on your floater from last week, your... Mary Frances Clarke? She was underwater for 60 hours – give or take – and this one's a drowning – she drowned in Card Sound, which is to say she went in alive."

Shit. I rocked my chair up, splashing coffee onto the top of my desk.

"I don't know whether she was conscious or unconscious," Madge Foster continued, "but she was alive. No evidence of sexual assault. Let's see...tox is clean. Um, you should know that there was a blunt-force trauma to the right temple not long before she died, within 12 hours. It was concussive, could have knocked her out, but that's not definitive. She went into the water very late Tuesday night, very early Wednesday morning, the wee hours. The fisherman witness who saw her on Friday must have seen her within an hour of her surfacing – I told you that – so there you have it. I'll close this report and have a copy sent your way. You got everything?"

"You're the best, Madge. I owe you one." I was still writing, trying to jot down what she was telling me.

"You owe me more than one, Segal. Sheena Easton's playing in Miami next month. You want to buy a pair of tickets and invite

14

your favorite ME?"

"I'm dialing Ticketron now."

"Uh-huh." She hung up.

I did owe her, and so did every detective in the county. I couldn't count the times that something in one of her reports had pointed me in a direction that my own examination of the victim did not suggest. Only this time, there were no helpful surprises, just an extra dose of horror. Mary Clarke had been alive when she sank into the bay, maybe even aware.

*   *   *

It was a little after 4:00 p.m. when I drove down Old Cutler Road, past Matheson Hammock and Fairchild Tropical Gardens, to 105th Street. That led to a posh neighborhood and because I was early for my meeting with Clarke, I drove around for a bit.

The homes were widely spaced, most sitting on lots of an acre or more. Many had circular drives, mostly occupied by Buicks and Volvos and such. I didn't see any Porsches or Benzes, guessing that the Porsche and Mercedes drivers were at work. Some homes, the more expensive ones, were hidden from the street, a mailbox and a drive that curved out of sight behind lush landscaping the only evidence of the residence.

The Clarke home was a visible one. In the driveway was a Mercury station wagon and a Jaguar sedan. I parked behind the wagon. After I rang the doorbell, and as the latch clicked and the weather-stripping began to peel apart, I heard someone call out, "No. Adam, no!" A towheaded boy about five or six years old pulled the door wide open. Roger Clarke was rushing behind the boy, skidding to a stop when he saw me. He exhaled with a puff and waved me inside. The boy backed up against his dad's legs.

Regaining his composure, he touched the boy's head and said, "Adam, this is Detective Segal. He's a policeman."

I stepped farther into the tiled foyer and did a deep knee bend to get eye-level with young Adam Clarke. "Pleased to meet you, Adam," I said. The feeling wasn't mutual. He spun around his dad and bolted out of the room. As I watched him go, he bounced off another pair of legs just entering the room, feminine legs.

From squat level the legs appeared impossibly long, but even when I stood, she was tall, close to six feet. She was dressed in short-shorts and a taut, brightly colored halter top.

"I'm sorry," she said, "I didn't hear the bell."

"That's okay. Marsha, this is Detective Segal. Detective, this is our neighbor, Marsha."

I nodded and smiled. Her features were plain but somewhere along the way she had learned how to emphasize her best ones. I was still taking in the flame-red hair framing a freckled face and wondering at encountering another woman in Mary Clarke's house when Roger Clarke read my mind and jumped in.

"Goodwin," he amended. "Marsha Goodwin. She lives next door and she has been looking after Cheri and Adam in the afternoons." He turned to her and added, "She's been a lifesaver."

That did help, but "lifesaver" struck me as an unfortunate word choice.

Marsha gave me an acknowledging nod, then turned, "Roger, I have to go home to check on dinner. Will you be finished here by six?"

Clarke looked at me and I gave a nod.

"Fine, come about then. Cheri's lying down in her room. You

will probably find Adam in the back of his closet."

Clarke thanked her and Marsha Goodwin turned to me.

"You'll find who killed Mary, Detective?"

"We'll do our best, Miss Goodwin." I was fishing with the Miss, but she didn't react.

"If I can help, any way at all, please ask."

I thanked her and she turned and left the room, apparently leaving the house through a back door.

Roger Clarke showed me into a large family room at the back of the house. One wall was all glass doors, the kind that slid out of the way to open the room completely to a patio and a pool covered by an immense domed screen enclosure. Today the doors were closed and cool air spilled out of overhead vents. A gigantic television occupied one inside corner of the room, turned on to a sports channel but muted. I imagined how good the Dolphins games would be on it.

Roger went to a wet bar on the opposite wall, turning to offer me a drink. I declined but he fixed himself something before taking the chair opposite the one I was in. He took a sip, then said, "Okay, what do you want to know?"

"I want to see where she was the last time anyone saw her. But first, I would like you to tell me exactly what happened Tuesday."

He looked puzzled, so I added, "The school called your office?"

"Yes."

"Were you alarmed?"

"Alarmed? You mean did I think something had happened to my wife? No, not really."

"Your wife often fails to pick up your children?"

"No. Never. But...I don't know. I assumed she had car trouble or fell asleep, here at home, something."

"Did you try calling home?"

"Yes."

I raised my eyebrows, waiting for more.

"No one answered."

"What time was that?"

"Right after the school called me, just before I left to go pick up the kids."

"Why did the school wait until three-forty to call you?" I was talking as much to myself as to him.

"I don't know. Maybe Cheri and Adam didn't say anything to anyone for a while. And I'm sure the school tried the home number a couple of times first before calling me."

"Were you in your office all afternoon?"

He sat back in the chair. "I left to pick up the kids."

"No. I'm asking if the school had called earlier, would you have been in your office?"

He sipped his drink. "I was in my office."

"*All* afternoon?"

"Anytime the school might have called."

"Meaning after three."

"Yes."

"What about between one-thirty and three? The pool service saw Mrs. Clarke at one-thirty, she's missing by three."

He didn't like the question. He put his glass down and considered me. "Why are you asking me that?"

I leaned back into a corner of the chair, cocked my head, and held his eyes for a moment. When I thought the pause had been long enough, I said, "I need to know where you were when your wife was murdered, Mr. Clarke."

"You think I killed my wife?"

"I don't know who killed your wife, but I intend to turn over every stone until I find something that helps me answer that question. I don't yet know much about you, Mr. Clarke. What I do already know is that spouses kill each other all the time. I'm not here in your nice home because I am a sympathetic friend or a helpful neighbor. I'm a cop, a dogged one, and I'm here looking for whoever killed Mary Frances Clarke. If you did have anything to do with your wife's death, I will find that out. If you didn't, your cooperation could help me to find out who did."

It was a fairly good speech, one I'd delivered before, but he didn't like it as much as I did.

He sat forward. "I had nothing to do with Mary's murder."

"Where were you between one-thirty and three."

"My office."

He was lying and so transparent at it that I thought this case might get wrapped up quickly. I made him wait and watch while I wrote down what he had just told me.

"After you tried calling home, then what happened?"

"I drove to the school and picked up the kids. Mary's car was here when we got home, so we all looked through the house and outside for her. She wasn't here. We waited a bit, but I knew something was wrong so I called the police. They wanted me to wait a while longer, but I raised hell and they sent someone quickly. The officer who came filled out a report. The next day, a detective came out."

"Her car was here?"

"Yes."

"And the house was locked?"

"The front door was, but the back was open."

"These doors?" I asked, nodding toward the sliding doors behind me.

"Yes."

"But everything else was locked?"

"No. The kitchen door was also unlocked and that end of the screen room wasn't latched."

"Show me."

The kitchen opened off one end of the family room. He flipped a wall switch as we entered and the entire ceiling illuminated. It was a big kitchen with an island in the middle. The cabinets were white, the countertops red tile. At the far end, Clarke opened the door for me. In addition to the regular lock set, it had a deadbolt up high.

I stepped through the door and onto a spacious covered patio. The pool didn't extend this far, and at this end, beyond brick columns, was a tropical garden.

"Which screen door was unlatched?" I asked.

"This one." He indicated the one close to my left.

I examined the latch, opened the door, and scanned the side yard where it led. When I released it, it latched automatically. There was a little button on the inside that someone would have to push to keep it from locking automatically when closed.

I turned to ask Clarke about the latch, but he had his back to me, his head cocked at an inquisitive tilt. I looked beyond him to see what had his attention. Past the sliding glass doors of the family room, a small door into the house was ajar. A strip of green cloth lay in front of the open door.

Roger Clarke started toward the open door, then he suddenly looked toward the pool. I was trying to look where he was looking when he said, "Oh God!" and hit full stride in two steps. I followed toward the near end of the pool where I finally saw what he had seen. At the deep end, on the bottom, lay a dark green object. I had no idea what it was, but Clarke must have known because he was already to the middle of the pool and in mid-air.

I ran forward as he breached the surface of the water and began struggling against the air trapped in his clothes to pull himself to the bottom of the pool. His shoes weren't helping. By the time he reached whatever was at the bottom, his clothes must have gone from flotation to ballast because he didn't come right back up. The water's surface was so disturbed that I couldn't see what he had, but then his hands burst through the surface pushing a bundle of green cloth with small limbs hanging from it. I caught my breath and felt my skin crawl. *Jesus!* I took the child from him, heavy and awkward. I cradled her, rolling her into my elbows as I backed away from the pool, laying her down. I peeled the cloth away. Her eyes were closed and she was completely still, non-responsive. The spill of hair across her forehead was the same shade of blonde as I had seen on a woman just days ago, lying on a bank of dead coral.

I grabbed her ankles and stood, lifting her, allowing as much water as possible to drain from her lungs. Roger Clarke gripped the coping of the pool, coughing up water and trying to breathe.

I laid the little girl back down on the deck and began to work on her, at first frantically, then methodically as my training took over. Between tries to force air into her lungs, I saw Clarke was still in the pool, paralyzed. "Clarke!" I yelled. "Nine-one-one! Call nine-one-one!"

He jerked himself free of the pool, bringing gallons of water out with him, and raced through the open door. I was aware of him on the phone, loud and urgent. A minute later, he was back.

"They're on their way."

I had her nose pinched and was blowing into her mouth. When I looked up, he had leaned against the wall and slid down to a seated position, defeated.

Then she coughed. A little burble, then another cough. I rolled her on her side and pounded her back. Her little body heaved, and water gushed out. She began to gasp between coughs. Her breathing finally settled down to a watery rasp, then she threw up. Clarke had crawled across the deck and was holding her forehead in one of his big hands. "Cheri, you're going to be okay, it's going to be okay." Big tears ran down his face and this time I did feel sorry for him. If he had gotten to her 30 seconds later, he would have been arranging two funerals in one week.

The open door led to a bathroom and through it was the master bedroom. I pulled the spread off the big bed and took it back out to the deck. We needed to keep her out of shock. Together, we got her out of the wet cloth and wrapped her in the spread. Her eyes were open, but she didn't speak. I wondered if her brain had been without oxygen for too long.

The green cloth turned out to be Mary Clarke's bathrobe. The tie had been what Roger first saw in front of the door. The girl had wrapped herself tightly in her dead mother's robe and stepped into the pool. She must have gone under just before we came out the kitchen door. I tried to remember what my life was like at 11 or 12. I was sure suicide wasn't even in my vocabulary at that age. The thought of someone this young filled with such despair left me with ample despair of my own. I was glad she had failed.

Emergency arrived and took over. Two patrolmen also showed up and the commotion brought little Adam out of hiding. When he saw his sister being strapped to the gurney, he took off again. Clarke went with the ambulance and I promised to round up Adam and get him over to Marsha Goodwin's. The driver told me they were taking her to Mercy.

*   *   *

Unable to coax Adam out of his closet, I left a patrolman in the house and went for Marsha Goodman. I had thought the commotion of the emergency vehicles might have brought her next door until I walked over and discovered her house was around the corner, facing the cross street.

When she answered her door and recognized me, she got a look on her face of someone expecting to hear bad news. I wondered if she was clairvoyant, but I didn't disappoint her. I told her about Cheri and she turned an unflattering shade of green. She invited me in and excused herself.

I had never been in a room quite like her living room. Only a small border of hardwood showed around the edge of the thick Persian rug. The rug itself was spectacular, but the furnishings really got my attention. I had no idea whether they were real antiques or copies sold by one of the big furniture warehouses out on the Palmetto Expressway. Either way, the room looked like it belonged in a European palace. A very ornate gold clock on the mantel struck. I glanced at my digital watch. The clock was eight minutes slow.

"Poor Cheri. Poor Roger." She had returned to the room.

"Mr. Clarke went to the hospital with her. He hoped you could look after Adam, but I couldn't bring him to you without adding to the trauma."

"Of course," she said. "Let me check the oven. Come this way. We'll go out the back."

I followed her through a high-tech kitchen, past a table set for four, and out French doors. Her pool was not screened and we crossed her lawn and through a gate into the Clarkes' side yard. The screen room door I had looked at earlier was latched, so we had to go around to the front to get into the house. She easily coaxed little Adam out of his closet and took him back to her house, to feed him dinner.

*   *   *

I found Roger Clarke in a small waiting room in the east wing of the hospital. He had his head in his hands, a hospital blanket over his shoulders, his wet jacket hung on the arm of the chair next to him, dripping slowly into a small puddle beneath it.

"How is she?"

He looked up. "I don't know. Waiting."

"Excuse me, sir." It was a voice from behind. I turned and moved out of a doorway I didn't realize I was blocking. A small woman in a white coat moved past me. She had a photo ID card clipped to her coat that said Dr. Zyne in bold letters.

"Mr. Clarke?"

Clarke stood quickly, suddenly animated. "I'm Mr. Clarke."

"We are going to admit her, Mr. Clarke, but Cheri is going to be fine. You can see her now if you like."

The two of them went back through the double doors into the emergency room and I turned to the uniform working on the suicide report to give him my statement. When he had everything he needed, I went to the gift shop for flowers, but bought a colorful balloon instead, and a small box of candy. Back at emergency, the desk nurse told me Cheri had been moved to a room. The number she gave me was on the fourth floor.

When I located it, the door was open. Roger Clarke was sitting on the bed. His bulk blocked any view of his little girl from the door. I thought how easy it would have been for a guy his size to pitch his little wife over that bridge railing. I knocked softly.

"Come in. Come in. We were just talking about you." He turned back to the bed and said, "Detective Segal is here."

As I appeared from behind her father and walked around to the other side of the bed, her eyes never left my face. Her distinctive blonde hair covered her pillow. The waxy complexion at the pool was replaced with some pinkness in her cheeks.

"I'm glad you're feeling better," I said, flinching at how horribly matter of fact that sounded, not at all reflecting how happy I really was to see her so alert. It was my breath that had restored her own. I had given her life. I wondered if what I was feeling was anything like how a woman feels having given birth. I certainly felt an impulse to protect this child, to guide her through the darkness that brought her here. Instead, I said, "These are for you." I laid the box of candy on the bed and tied the balloon to the nightstand drawer handle.

"Thank you," she said in a hoarse voice. She looked at her

father, then back at me.

I nodded. She seemed older here than the child at the pool. I wondered how she was feeling about what she had tried to do. *Don't do that again!* I thought, but did not say. Then another thought came, unwanted. *Whoever laced her mother to that block and dropped her off the bridge might well draw the death penalty. Had I restored this girl's life only to eventually make her an orphan?* I shook that thought from my brain and gave her my best smile.

*   *   *

It was close to 8:00 p.m. and the sun was still up when I got back to the station. I stopped by the break room for a cup of coffee from a pot brewed hours earlier. Bad coffee aside, I liked this time of day. With the regular shift bustle long over and no one dropping by my desk, it allowed for quiet contemplation of a case, for mentally organizing what I knew and what I didn't know.

The ME report on Mary Clarke was in my in-box. I sat down and thumbed through it quickly, seeing in print what Madge had shared on the phone.

Cause of Death: asphyxiation by drowning. Mary Frances Clarke was alive when she hit the water. She hadn't just been disposed of at the bridge, she had been murdered there.

Post-Mortem Interval: 60 hours. Mary Clarke went missing on Monday afternoon, but she did not end up in the bay until maybe early Tuesday morning. Where was she in the meantime?

I finished reading the report and then pulled out my notebook and wrote in it the four pieces of information from the report that summarized about all I knew about her murder so far: No drugs, not raped, trauma – right temple, drowned.

The first item on that list did not rule out the possibility that her murder was somehow drug related. Increasingly the murders I investigate have something to do with drugs. All the autopsy report told me was that Mary Frances Clarke was a healthy woman in her thirties who did not have any drugs in her system.

The autopsy had also failed to reveal any signs of rape. No traces of semen, no bruises or abrasions, no evidence of sodomy, no skin cells from her attacker under her nails. This was consistent with what I had seen at the bridge. It seemed unlikely that a rapist would put her bathing suit back on her before tying her to a block for her final dip. I was satisfied that she had her top on, too, when she went in. Rape did not fit as a motive.

She had taken a heavy blow to the right side of her head, contusions and evidence of swelling marking the blow as happening prior to her death by drowning. I flipped through the photographs until I found the ones of Mary Clarke's feet. The neat wrap of the cord argued against her being aware of what was happening to her. No, someone had struck Mary Clarke in the head, knocking her unconscious and allowing that person or someone to lace her obliging ankles neatly and methodically to that block. I wanted to make something of the fact that the blow was to her right temple, but I couldn't. The attacker might have been left-handed, but the blow could have been swung backhand. Or maybe she had her back to the attacker. I moved on. All the report gave me was that she had taken a blow to the head from a blunt object.

It was the last item on my list, death by drowning, which gave me the most difficulty, not because of any lack of conclusiveness but because of the horrifying implications. A concrete block and a ball of twine as a means of disposal has a certain warped logic to it, but when I thought of those two items as a murder weapon, it made my blood run cold. I had not told her husband. There was no point in adding to his grief. Or perhaps he already knew.

*   *   *

It had rained while I was inside. The wet streets multiplied the already extravagant lights of Miami, making them even more beautiful, but the jeweled lady can have a black heart. While I drove home, go-fast boats were coasting up to darkened docks with consignments of cocaine, cargo planes at Miami International were loading illegal weapons bound for Nicaragua, bankers were adjusting the books and reserving flights on Swissair, hookers were leaving mid-western businessmen in 79th Street motels with a smile and no wallet, teenagers high on crack were stealing CD players from their neighbors, and someone was wondering whether they had left any tracks when they tossed a little blonde housewife off a south Dade bridge.

Of course, the tracks are there; they always are. If I failed to find them, it will be because I didn't look in the right place. When I stretched out on my bed at home, I assured myself I had just gotten started. My thoughts were drifting from the ME report to the cord, then to the block, examining every side of it, something about it, when sleep slipped in and turned off the projector.

I woke up falling, heart racing, skin tingling. But it wasn't me falling, it was Pam. From Card Sound Bridge. Had I pushed her over the rail? And why Pam? We haven't been married for eight years, haven't seen each other in six. Then her face changed to Cheri Clarke, looking up at me as she fell away from the bridge. I reached down and down for her, but she didn't reach back. Wrapped tightly in green, she disappeared into blackness.

I took several deep breaths, consciously willing my world back into place. Across the dark room, the alarm clock on the desk, there to keep its snooze button out of reach, showed 2:35 in four-inch red numbers. I got up, turned on the desk light and pulled the telephone book from the bottom drawer. When I found the number, I dialed it, asking for the fourth-floor nurses' station.

I asked the person on the other end of the line how Cheri Clarke was doing.

"Let me give you her nurse," she said.

A man's voice said, "Good morning. Kind of early. And what is your relationship?"

"I'm her uncle," I said, "and yeah, I can't sleep. How is she?"

It must have been a slow night because he said, "Let me check." He was soon back on the phone assuring me that my "niece" was sleeping peacefully.

I returned to bed and slept dreamless for the remainder of the night, until my alarm sounded at 6:30, but I did not feel rested.

4

WEDNESDAY, MORNING

THE SKY SHOWED NO TRACE of the night's rain, but my own clouds had not cleared. I poured up a bowl of cereal and covered it with milk.

The front page of the newspaper showed a picture of the same athlete who smiled at me from the cereal box, only in the newspaper photo he was not smiling. He had been arrested for supplying his teammates with cocaine. He was making six million for playing and who knows how much in endorsements and that still left him short? I let him bear the brunt of my stormy mood. I wanted to see him locked up as long as possible. And when he got out, I wanted to know that no team would ever sign him, except to clean the stadium after the games.

Of course, none of that was going to happen. I knew that the next time I saw this face it would be on TV, and he would be in uniform, out on the field, the commentators talking about his "difficult time" as though he had caught a bum rap. He wasn't really dealing, they would say. He was a victim of the onerous pressures faced by professional athletes, but he'd endured. They would praise his recovery. Recovery from what? From greed? From moral deficiency? From social contempt? I felt sorry for the kids. They need better heroes.

I called the hospital again and got another good report on

Cheri Clarke. When I knew more, I might need to talk to her about her mother's murder – about her father too – but it was too soon and she was too fragile. Anyway, I would probably hand this task off. I was sure the hospital was going to hook her up with a counselor before releasing her. Maybe that person could help me assess Cheri's ability to help us. But protecting her from additional pain was going to have the upper hand in any decisions I made about Cheri Clarke.

I wanted to resume my conversation with Roger Clarke, but I reconsidered. In the last two days, the man had been informed of his wife's horrifying death, an undernourished civil servant had hinted that he was a murder suspect, and his 13-year-old daughter had attempted to take her own life. I could give him a day off with his children.

Before I left the house, I called the morgue. Someone there told me which funeral home had called for Mary Clarke's body. I called the funeral home and found out that the service was set for Friday afternoon. I jotted the time in my notebook and then went out to my car.

*   *   *

Pristine Pools is located way out Kendall Drive. I got there just before 10:00 and a bell announced my entry. Business was already in full swing and the place smelled strongly of chlorine. An older woman in the back was complaining about yellow water to a young guy holding a pool-water tester up to the light. At the counter, a young girl was stacking up various plastic buckets and jars for a woman with a preschooler on each hand. The guy and the young girl both wore blue polo shirts with Pristine Pools embroidered on the fronts.

My focus was on a pink hot tub displayed at the front of the store when the young girl approached, "May I help you?"

"Is Greg Devereaux around?" During the missing person investigation, Sanchez had learned that it was Devereaux who had cleaned the Clarke pool on the afternoon that Mary Clarke disappeared. He had talked with Devereaux by phone and confirmed that Mrs. Clarke had been at home at 1:30 when he was servicing the pool. I needed to talk to Greg Devereaux in person.

"Um, no, he isn't. Can I help you?"

"When will he be in?"

"Um, he's out on his rounds. I guess this afternoon."

Behind the counter, a CB radio squawked to life. She excused herself and went to it. I waited while she spoke into the mike, confirming an address for someone. I walked over to the counter and when she replaced the mike, I asked, "Can you reach Devereaux on that?"

Her jaw tightened and she looked me over more closely. "I don't think I...does Greg know you?"

I showed her my badge. "No, he doesn't. I'm investigating a homicide, a Pristine Pools' customer."

She nodded solemnly, "Mrs. Clarke." Her response didn't surprise me. The victim's name and photo had made the evening news on Monday night. It would have been the number one topic of conversation at Pristine Pools since Tuesday. Also at Mary Clarke's dentist, baker, and hairdresser. "It's awful. But Greg said you already talked to him."

"Another detective talked with him. Can you reach him on the radio?"

"No. He does a fixed route. He doesn't have a radio in his truck."

"When you say a fixed route, does that mean he would be at the Clarke residence every Tuesday about one?"

"Um, maybe not right at one, but pretty much the same time every week, yeah."

"Do you know where he is today, now?"

"Um..."

I didn't know why she was hesitating, maybe nerves, but she finally pulled a loose-leaf notebook up from beneath the counter and thumbed through the pages before stopping and writing down an address.

"How about giving me the addresses for the appointments before and after that one?"

"Sure." She wrote two additional addresses.

"Thanks."

The lady with the yellow pool water was still bending the ear of the young guy in the back when the bell announced my exit. It was good to get back into the outside air.

I drove to the first address on the list and found the Pristine Pools truck parked in the driveway. It was a nice house in one of the new neighborhoods near the south campus of Dade County Junior College. Rather than ring the bell and ask for the pool man, I parked across the street and waited. After about 30 minutes passed with no sign of Devereaux, I put down my newspaper and considered the scene. There was no other vehicle in the drive and the garage door was closed. The house sat on a large corner lot. I started my car and idled slowly around the corner.

A wall blocked any view of the backyard, where the pool

presumably was. I parked and quietly got out of the car. At the corner of the wall was a wrought-iron gate that opened into a small alcove for the garbage cans. Through the gate I could see the pool. No one was cleaning it. The deck was dry. I walked around to the front of the house. The truck was still there.

I turned to the sound of a car behind me, a green and white Metro squad car. Someone in the neighborhood had called about me, a stranger creeping around. I didn't know the officer, but I showed him a badge and he took off. I went back to my car, drove around to where I had parked before, and waited.

I had been there over an hour when the garage door opened. A little red convertible, an Alfa Romeo I think, backed out. I couldn't tell much about the blonde woman in dark glasses behind the wheel, except that she went well with the car.

Devereaux finally appeared about 20 minutes after she drove off. He was the lifeguard type: blonde, tan, and fit. He had some of his pool cleaning equipment with him and he was putting it in the truck when I approached, walking up the driveway.

"Greg Devereaux?"

"Yeah."

"I'm a police officer, Mr. Devereaux, Detective Segal. I'm investigating the death of Mrs. Mary Clarke and I have a few questions for you."

"Yeah, okay. But I already talked with another detective... Fernandez maybe."

"Sanchez."

"Sanchez, yeah." He nodded as he spoke.

He was young, early- to mid-twenties. He was my height, but his arms were bigger than my legs and the sleeves of the blue Pristine Pools pullover were pushed up above his biceps. His head was covered in loose sun-bleached curls. He'd also been blessed with a square jaw and pale green eyes. He made me think beach movie, or yacht crew. It wasn't going to be easy for me to like Greg Devereaux.

"I have some additional questions. How about we get a cup of coffee?"

"Um..."

"I talked to your boss at the shop, you can take the time. There's a Dixie Donuts two blocks from here, you know it? I'll follow you."

"I got equipment to put away, but yeah."

I nodded. "Not a problem, I'll wait."

In the open neck of the pullover, he sported two gold chains. A pair of designer sunglasses rested on his chest, suspended by a leather thong under the collar. His left wrist carried a gold Rolex.

It didn't take him long to clean up and I was soon sitting across from him in the donut shop, a Bavarian creme long john on a plate in front of me. I could feel my arteries protesting as I ate. Devereaux had only black coffee.

"Tell me about Tuesday of last week."

"I do the Clarke pool on Tuesdays. Mrs. Clarke was out by the pool when I got there. When I started, she went into the house. I cleaned the pool and I left. That was about one-thirty. That's it, just like I told...uh, the other detective."

"What was she wearing?"

"A bathing suit."

"Can you describe it?"

He flicked his left hand as we talked, repositioning the Rolex.

"I don't know." He sat back in the booth and tilted his head up. "It was a two piece, a bikini." He looked back at me and shook his head. "I don't remember what it looked like."

I had the bottom in a bag in my pocket. I pulled the bag out and set it on the table between us. "Could this have been the suit she was wearing?"

He was looking at the suit and I was looking at him. He made no attempt to pick up the bag. After a little bit too long, he said, "Maybe."

"You don't remember?"

"I've seen a bathing suit like that, but I'm not sure I saw it on Mrs. Clarke."

"It's what she had on when we found her," I volunteered.

"Then it's probably what I saw on Mrs. Clark. I'm just not sure."

"Fair enough." I put the plastic bag back in my pocket. "You called her Mrs. Clarke, Greg?"

"What?"

"When you talked to her, you didn't call her Mary?"

"Uh, no, Mrs. Clarke."

"Was there anyone else at the house while you were there?"

"I didn't see anyone."

"Did the doorbell ring? The telephone?"

He shook his head side-to-side. "I don't know. It could have and I still wouldn't know, I...I just don't remember any details from that stop, that day, I didn't know...I didn't know it would matter."

"So, nothing unusual? Nothing?"

His neat hands turned palm up. "I got there. I serviced the

pool. I left."

"How long were you there?"

"I don't know, probably 40, 45 minutes."

"Is that how long it takes to service a pool?"

"A pool like the Clarkes', yeah, it's a big pool."

I finished my coffee, but I held the cup in both hands and looked over the top of it at Greg Devereaux.

"Greg, you understand that when Detective Sanchez talked with you, he was investigating a missing person. Mary Clarke was missing. It's not a crime to be missing. Maybe she had decided to leave. Maybe she and her husband had a fight. Maybe she took a cab to the airport to go visit her mother in Des Moines. Maybe she ran off with a lover."

I paused, put the cup down, and leaned forward on my elbows. "But she's no longer missing. I'm investigating a murder. Someone attached a weight to Mary Clarke and sunk her body in 12 feet of water. As far as we know, you are the last person who saw her alive. That isn't always significant, but it can be." I waited, noting his discomfort and letting it sink in before continuing. I had his full attention. "Did you ever have sex with Mary Clarke?"

"No."

I expected him to bristle a little, but he was as cool as a late afternoon in November, not a flicker in those pale green eyes. He looked relieved that the question was so easy.

"How about other customers? Do you sometimes play around with the lady of the house?" I heard a little sarcasm slip into my voice.

He heard it, too, and decided to go on the offensive. "Look, I don't know who the hell you think you are, or what you're trying

to suggest. I go to people's houses and I take care of their swimming pools. That's what I do." He paused, deciding who had the
juice here. "Not that it's any of your fucking business. I have to
go." He slid to the edge of the seat and hoisted himself to his feet.

"Sit down, Devereaux," I barked. "I'm not done." He turned
to respond, but I cut him off. "We can finish this here, or we can
do it over squad-room coffee, your choice."

He remained standing for a couple of clicks, then slid back
into the booth. "I've told you everything I know. There's nothing
more I can give you."

"Everything? I don't think so." I allowed a slight smile on
my face.

"What are you talking about?"

I dropped the smile. "I sat out in front of the house where
I met you this morning for 90 minutes."

"It's a big pool…"

"But nobody was cleaning it."

He took a big breath and glanced away. "She's the only one."

I reached across the table and pressed the two gold chains
against his neck with my index finger, my eyes locked on his.
"This lady you serviced today might be good for a gold chain or
two, but a gold Rolex…?" I paused like I was considering something, shaking my head. "No, the Rolex is from a pool owner
in Gables Estates or Cocoplum." I stopped again, removed my
finger from his chest and held it up, like an aha moment, "Or
Mary Clarke's neighborhood. Did Mary give you that watch?"

I'd gone out on a limb, uncomfortably far, but it was the only
way to see if it held. Sometimes it breaks, sometimes you pick fruit.

Greg glanced down at his wrist, "I bought this watch," the

emphasis on I.

"Yeah? You own Pristine Pools? Or you got another source of income, something I shouldn't know about? Ten-grand watches leave a trail, Greg. Finding out which pool lady gave it to you will be easy. We've got a properties team at the station who..."

"They come on to me." It was almost a whine, the bluster gone now.

"Did you have something going with Mary Clarke?" He flicked his left hand. Twice. He was nervous. I wondered if it was because he was about to lie to me again. Or was he going to tell me the truth, but he was afraid that I would think it was a lie. Or he was afraid of the truth. If I could read minds, it would make my job easier.

"No."

"Never?"

"Never."

"You come out once a week. You clean the pool. You're gone in 45 minutes. The neighbors and your other Tuesday appointments aren't going to tell me anything that contradicts that?"

"I'm telling the truth. I never made it with Mrs. Clarke. Never! Christ, if this'd happened on any other day of the week, I wouldn't be involved."

"Tuesday is as good a day as any, don't you think, to get killed and leave your two young kids without a mother." I regretted it as soon as I said it, but he'd pissed me off. His only feeling about the death of Mary Clarke was that it was putting his little playhouse at risk.

I was almost satisfied he was telling the truth, but I grilled him another 10 minutes just to harass him. His story didn't change. He left at about 1:30 and Mary Clarke was still alive, doing something in the kitchen.

We left the donut shop together. I let him know I'd be talking to him again, though I had no reason to believe I would. My car was beyond his truck, so I stepped out into the lot to go behind it, scanning the bed as I walked by. It held a large tank mounted behind the cab, likely filled with chlorine. Poles, brushes, nets, and hoses lay scattered on top of a dozen plastic containers. There were sections of plastic pipe and assorted fittings. As I walked past, I saw in the back corner of the bed, up against the tailgate, two concrete blocks. I circled my car and went back into the donut shop.

They hadn't bussed the table. There was a short, bald guy behind the counter and I told him I needed a good heavy cup for coffee in the office; would he sell me one? He set a clean one on the counter and rang me up.

"I'll just take the one I've already used," I said, nodding toward the booth.

"Suit yourself."

I paid him, then turned to look out the windows. The Pristine Pools truck was gone. I went back to the booth, moved my cup to Devereaux's side of the table, put my hand inside his cup, spread my fingers, and picked it up.

5

WEDNESDAY, AFTERNOON

WAYNE THOMAS WAS SITTING IN MY desk chair chewing on a plastic straw. When he saw me coming, I could tell he was eager to unload something on me. "Rolando Ortega. We picked him up coming out of a house on 144th at two in the afternoon with a full pillowcase. We went to his house, packed with jewelry, silver, cameras, electronics." He paused for effect, waiting for me to bite. I focused on the fast-food trash that wasn't mine, filling my wastepaper basket. He continued. "Most of the stuff we checked came from a couple of recent burglaries. Care to guess where they were?"

Wayne likes to do this. He always wants to tell you about the case he's working on, but he wants to tell it like you're playing Charades. Wayne is a nice guy and a hell of a good cop, but I just didn't need any more puzzles. I humored him anyway. "The mayor's house?"

"Noooo...c'mon Segal."

"Come on Wayne." I waved him out of my chair. "I don't have time for this. Just give it to me. Or don't."

He moved to the side chair, giving me his injured look. "I'm trying to help you out here."

I ignored him, flipping the switch on my Selectric and

pulling some blank paper from the middle drawer. I wanted to transcribe my conversation with Devereaux while it was still fresh.

"Alright, look. One was on 101st Street, another one on 56th Avenue."

"Um." I'd flipped open my notebook to review what I'd written down while Greg spoke. It wasn't much.

"Neither house is more than three blocks from where the late Mary Clarke resided."

That got me to look up. "A burglar?"

"Why not? This Ortega is a sleaze. Say he slipped into the back of the house and ran into Mrs. Clarke. She screams, picks up the phone or whips out a .357, I don't know. He panics and hits her."

"Her car was in the driveway, Wayne. This Ortega have a record of targeting occupied houses in the middle of the afternoon?"

Wayne chewed a little harder on the straw. "Maybe the car wasn't there, maybe she was out for an errand and came home to catch him in the act."

I considered Wayne's burglary-turned-murder theory, then shook my head. "What, they have this surprise encounter, she's knocked out and he doesn't run? No, he hauls her out of the house to his car, parked somewhere else – and this in broad daylight – then drives her 30 miles south, waits until dark, ties a block to her, and tosses her off a bridge? Makes no sense."

He nodded thoughtfully, then leaned back and crossed his arms behind his head. Wayne is from a small town in Georgia, and I knew I was in for a dose of down-home wisdom, delivered in his distinctive drawl.

"When I was about so high," he held his hand out about waist level, "Daddy bought me a BB gun. Mama didn't like it. First couple months, I was on my best behavior, broke every bottle and dented every can that came out of the kitchen, but not once did I point the gun at anyone. I didn't sting one of the cows, break a window, or in any way give my folks cause to worry. Mama even came to like that gun because it kept me out of her hair for hours at a stretch."

I sat back in surrender.

"There was a big red cardinal on the place," Wayne continued, "and Mama dearly loved to see that bird from the kitchen window. One day I was out by the barn with my gun and that dang cardinal landed nearby. I shot at the fence post it was on, just to scare it, but my shot went high and the bird fell dead. Now, birds don't much bleed, not unless you shoot 'em in the head, so the wound from my BB woulda been near impossible to find because of the feathers. I shoulda just left the bird there on the ground by the fence where it landed and my folks woulda chalked it up to a hawk or the cat or something. But that ain't what I did."

He paused long enough to uncross his arms and stretch them above his head.

"Wayne..."

"No. What I did was tie a rock to its little feet and toss it into our pond."

I shook my head and turned back to the Selectric.

"Ok, maybe not," Wayne agreed. "What I did do is sneak it away from the house and bury it in the woods. Point is, after I killed that bird, I didn't want anyone to find it. I knew if they asked me about it, my face would give me away."

"No body, no murder. That's your burglar's reason for removing Mary Clarke's body from the home?"

"With your mind, Stick, criminals just don't stand a chance."

"Did you get away with it?" I asked, knowing I shouldn't.

"Yes and no." He waited, but I was done so he continued. "Next morning, the bird was on the porch, all chewed up. My dog had seen me bury it. Of course, Mama thought Bandit had killed it and she whupped that dog something awful. He was my best friend and I didn't stop her. I didn't much like myself for a long time after that."

"You mention Mary Clarke to Ortega?"

"No. I just got this match with the loot a couple hours ago. You're probably right about Ortega, but you got anybody else?"

I laced my fingers behind my head. "I don't know. The pool guy was the last person to see her alive and I've got this tiny window between when he saw her and when she couldn't be reached. This cat's a real Casanova, servicing more than the pools on his route. He's sporting jewelry, shades, and a watch that a pool cleaner salary can't be paying for. He says Mary Clarke wasn't in his stable. Maybe, maybe not. And every time I see her husband, there's a beautiful woman nearby. Maybe they were both playing around. My interview with the husband was interrupted before we got very far, but he was guarded right from the start. There is something off about him that I need to know more about."

Wayne pushed himself to his feet. "Does kinda sound domestic," he agreed, "but it couldn't hurt to take a run at my burglar."

*   *   *

Rolando Ortega was a small guy, maybe five feet six. Mexican. Or maybe Colombian. Mid-twenties, greasy hair, bad complexion.

unkempt. He sat at one side of a long gray metal table, looking agitated and unhappy. Wayne was already a few minutes into the interview.

I took a seat at the near end of the table. Ortega's assigned public defender sat at the opposite end, like he didn't want to get too close to his client. He was writing something inside his open briefcase. I remembered doing math homework in history class and wondered if the attorney was catching up on paperwork from other cases. Not that I cared. You catch a guy coming out of someone's house with a bag of jewelry, then find that guy's house filled with stolen stuff, there shouldn't be a defense.

"I told you, man, I never stole nothing. Guy gave me a bunch a shit to sell. I don't know where he got it, I'm just sellin' the shit."

"Door-to door?" Wayne tilted his head, then smiled like he was finally understanding something he'd been confused about. "Okay, okay, I got it. You're like those Avon ladies, only you carry your goods in a pillowcase. Makes sense, like maybe we owe you an apology." Wayne stopped talking and stared at Ortega. Ortega's English was faulty, but he understood mockery. He just stared back.

"The thing is, Rolando," Wayne continued, "the arresting officers caught you coming out of a house belonging to Mr. and Mrs. Richards. You say you were there just trying to sell them some of your special shit your guy gave you. But the problem is – a problem for you, not for me – is that the pillowcase you got all your special shit in, that's Mr. Richards' pillowcase. I say Mr. Richards because my daddy always slept on the side of the bed closest to the door. You sleep on that side? Don't answer, I got off track." Wayne was in full theatrical mode and I was trying to keep a smile from creeping onto my face.

"Point is," Wayne continued, "I think you're a pillowcase thief. And it gets worse. 'Cause all that special shit you were trying to sell to the Richards, all of it is the Richards' special shit, from their special house."

"They're lyin'. They just after my shit without payin'."

"I could see that. I mean, it is nice stuff." Wayne paused and nodded. "Yeah, so nice Rolando, so very nice, that the Richards long ago took photographs of every single item for their insurance company."

Ortega tried again. "I never in that house. The cops lie. Nobody saw me come out of no house. If that shit stolen, wasn't me." He looked toward the public defender.

At Wayne's assertion of photographs, the attorney had extracted a yellow pad from his briefcase and was filling a few lines with notes. He met Ortega's gaze and gave him a reassuring nod.

I cleared my throat to draw attention, then pushed the folder in front of me toward Wayne's side of the table. Wayne picked it up.

"Mr. Ortega, I'm Detective Frank Segal. I'm sorry you're in this fix, and I get it. You have to be so careful today or someone will steal everything you've worked so hard to get. No one knows this better than Detective Thomas and I am sure he is going to do everything he can to help you out and get this misunderstanding cleared up."

Ortega had lost the thread now and was looking at me with more curiosity than concern. Wayne moved around me to Ortega's side of the table.

"Meanwhile, maybe you can give me a little help," I continued.

I gave Wayne a nod and he dropped the folder on the table

in front of Ortega, then opened it. Ortega looked down at the eight-by-ten color photo of Mary Clarke, the photo that Roger Clarke had given to the officer who responded when he reported her missing. I was thinking of Wayne's unintentional murder of the cardinal and I kept my eyes locked on Ortega's face. It betrayed nothing.

"You remember her?"

He looked up when I spoke, then down at the photo again. "I never seen that lady."

"You sure? Take a close look. She's on your route."

He shook his head. "No. Never seen her."

"It's Rolando, right?" I leaned toward him and pointed at the photo. "Well, Rolando, someone walked in through the back door of this pretty lady's house last week and killed her. Around two in the afternoon. Two o'clock, that's about when you make your sales calls in this lady's neighborhood. You see what I'm getting at here?"

The defense attorney was paying more attention now. Careers are built on murder cases, not run-of-the-mill burglaries. He folded a page of his yellow pad behind to expose a fresh sheet.

Ortega was paying attention, too. He held his hands up, palms out. "I never seen that lady," he said – for the third time.

"No? You know what forensics is, Rolando? That's where we look for fingerprints and hair and stuff. You sure our forensics guys won't find something small that shows you were in this lady's house? You didn't touch anything when you were in the house, leave a hair behind?"

"Wasn't in her house."

"That's good to hear," I said. "I mean, you're already in trouble here, Rolando. I don't think Detective Thomas believes you about this burglary thing. Tell me, are you an American citizen?

Wayne shook his head.

"No. See, that might just be a good thing, Rolando, because even if he pins it on you, a judge might just put you on a plane and send you home. But murder, Rolando, that's different. That could mean the chair. You never go home."

"This not right." he protested. "I don't know nothing about that lady."

"Now if it was an accident," I went on, "say someone was in her house and she came home and found that person there, and that person pushed her trying to run away. And say she fell and hit her head. If that's how it happened, you need to tell us now, because later a jury is never going to believe you. Is that how it happened, Rolando? Was it an accident?"

"I never push nobody. I never hurt nobody, ever. This shit wrong." Ortega looked toward the attorney but, pen down now, he was just listening.

"Never seen the woman in the picture?"

"No."

"Never in her house?"

"No."

"You're sure?"

He didn't respond.

"We're searching the house now, Rolando. Really thoroughly. If we find a hair of yours, a thread that matches one of your shirts. Or if a single item at your house belonged to this lady, odds are you're on your way to death row. You sure you don't want to tell me about it?"

Still no response. I stared him down for a minute, then stood and reached out for the open folder, closing it, and turning toward the door. Halfway there, I stopped and turned around. "You know anything about rich women, Rolando? Probably not. To a rich woman a thousand-dollar pair of earrings, a five-thousand-dollar watch, doesn't mean anything. She might easily loan them to a friend, a neighbor, somebody else on your route. If you do have that lady's earrings, it's not a coincidence a jury is likely to believe. They're going to convict you anyway. And you can bet that her borrowing friend, whose jewelry you did steal, isn't going to be interested in saving the ass of some scum low-life."

"Hey!" The defense objected.

I turned to the attorney. "Do your client a favor. Advise him of the value of the whole truth in his situation."

I turned back to Ortega. "Last chance, Rolando."

"This wrong," he repeated, staring down at the spot where the folder had been.

6

THURSDAY, MORNING

THE RECEPTIONIST SAID SHE WOULD CONNECT ME. A woman's voice followed, "Mr. Clarke's office."

"Mr. Clarke, please."

"He's not in the office today. Could someone else help you?"

"Miss del Portillo?"

"Yes?"

"Miss del Portillo, this is Frank Segal, I'm..."

"The detective."

"That's right."

"How can I help you?"

"Will Mr. Clarke be out of the office for the rest of the week?"

"Yes, he will."

"I called his home, but there was no answer."

"I think he's at the hospital, Detective."

"Of course. If he calls in, would you ask him to give me a call?"

"I'll be sure to give him the message. He checks in regularly."

I gave her my number and she repeated it back. I thanked her and was about to hang up.

"Detective?" Her voice had lost its sureness.

"Yes?"

"I, uh...I just wanted you to know how much Mr. Clarke

appreciates what you did Tuesday. He knows he would have lost his daughter if you hadn't been there. That would have killed him. Thank you."

I felt a warmth in my face, understanding that the thank you was from Miss del Portillo, not on behalf of Roger Clarke. "Mr. Clarke saved his daughter's life, Miss del Portillo. If he had noticed her seconds later, had been a little slower getting to her, nothing I could have done would have made any difference."

"But what you did made a difference. All the difference."

"Well, I'm glad there wasn't another death in the family."

There was a long silence at her end. When she finally spoke, her voice had lost all strength. "Detective, Mr. Clarke didn't kill his wife."

"He's not been accused."

"I know…" The control had returned to her voice. "But I want you to know that I am certain he is not responsible."

"How are you certain?"

"I know Mr. Clarke."

"I see. And I appreciate that, Miss del Portillo. For his sake – for Cheri's sake – I hope you're right."

After I hung up, I replayed the conversation in my mind several times. I had an uneasy feeling that Miss del Portillo had information that I could use, but I was quite sure that if it reflected badly on Roger Clarke, she would give it up only under the most desperate of circumstances.

*   *   *

It was just after noon when I took Devereaux's bagged coffee cup down two floors to Forensics. Jürgen Horkheimer was at his desk, dwarfing the chair underneath him. I told him what I was looking for, a full sweep of the Clarke residence, then added, "Could you do it today if I can get it set up?"

"Unless something else comes in."

"Great." I set the cup on his desk. "Name's Greg Devereaux." I watched him start to fill out the card. "E-A-U-X, yeah. Thanks. I'll check in later."

I continued downstairs to my car and took the Dolphin Expressway to I-95. South of downtown, more new high-rises were going up along Brickell Avenue. The national news magazines keep writing about the crime and drugs and immigrants in South Florida, about how nobody wants to come here anymore, but somebody must want to. The skyline is constantly changing. One local journalistic wit started a drive to make the construction crane Miami's official bird.

As soon as I turned onto Bayshore Drive, new construction was left behind. Canopied with huge oak and banyan trees, Bayshore runs alongside a wall that has been there for most of this century. Behind it are extensive Italian Renaissance gardens surrounding Villa Vizcaya, James Deering's 1916 estate. Shortly beyond the end of the wall, I turned into a drive that led to Mercy Hospital.

The free lot is the farthest from the door and I managed to find a partially shaded spot next to a young tree. For a minute I just sat in the car staring at nothing. I had come here to see Roger Clarke, to move this investigation along before the murderer died of old age. I had also come to see Cheri Clarke.

I was frightened for her; frightened at how short her life might have been – might still be. I was even frightened at how empty a long life might be and the part I might play in that. Part of her life was already gone, bloated and disfigured, lying on dead turtle grass. I had not known about Cheri then. I hoped she'd find the strength she was going to need to get through this.

My thoughts switched to my own mother. I sat in this same lot the night she died, sad at her loss, happy at her release from pain. The day before, I had cried at her side, telling her I was sorry about the lack of grandchildren. She had tried weakly to assure me her life had been rich in other ways.

Was it the heat rising from the black asphalt giving everything a teary distortion? Through the blur I could see potential conflict ahead. I wanted Wayne to find Mary Clarke's wedding ring among Ortega's cache. I wanted Horkheimer to find Greg Devereaux's fingerprints all over Mary Clarke's bedroom. I knew that when I found the tracks the murderer had left behind, if they led back to Roger Clarke, I would take myself off the case. I wouldn't be the guy to take Cheri's father away from her.

*   *   *

Ten minutes later I was back on South Bayshore driving through Coconut Grove. Her room had been empty. The duty nurse said that she had been released that morning and had left with her father.

The Mercury wasn't in the driveway, but the Jaguar was. I parked beside it. Roger Clarke answered the door and invited me in. I asked how she was doing.

"Come see."

I followed him through the dining room and the family room and into the kitchen. She was wearing pink jeans and a beige T-shirt. She was standing on her right leg, her left knee in a chair. Her back was to us, and she was bent over the table in deep concentration.

"Cheri, someone's here."

She turned and flashed a weak smile. "Hello, Detective Segal."

The T-shirt had a design on the front that said Rick's American Cafe. I smiled at that. *Of all the gin joints in all the world….*

She looked drawn, the smile forced. She was a young girl just out of the hospital who in 24 hours would be sitting front row at her mother's funeral. I forced my own smile, incongruous with the sense of foreboding I felt for her. "You look better than when I saw you last."

"Yeah, I know. I'm sorry."

That was not where I wanted the conversation to go. I nodded at the spread of jigsaw puzzle pieces on the table behind her. "That looks like it will take a while."

She turned back to it. "I know. Dad bought it for me. It's flamingos. Two thousand pieces!"

"Wow," I said. "Too many for me."

Roger Clarke and I went back to the family room, leaving Cheri to strain her eyes over differing shades of pink. I told Clarke that I wanted a team of technicians to come out this afternoon and process the house. He resisted the timing at first, needing a break for both him and his kids, but when I pointed out that people dropping by the following day, after the funeral, could spoil our chance of learning something, he relented. I called Horkheimer and gave him the green light.

"Alright, they're coming," I said when I put the receiver

down. "Meanwhile, maybe we can pick up where we left off?" I had opened my notebook to the notes I had been making when he spotted Cheri in the pool.

He nodded.

"Okay, the front was locked, the back was open. Mrs. Clarke was gone. Any signs of a struggle, anything out of place?

"No."

"Was a telephone off the hook? Anything lying on the floor?"

"No, nothing. The maid had been here on Monday, everything was still neat and clean. There were bowls and boxes and things on the kitchen counter, ingredients for something Mary was making. Nothing spilled or knocked over or anything. More like she was just getting started when..."

"The maid comes every Monday?" I interrupted. I had not thought about a maid.

"Yeah, mid-morning...oh." He had seen the look on my face. The maid had cleaned the house since Mary Clarke's disappearance.

"She can't have wiped everything" I said, then shrugged. We'll see what the team finds. Do you know what Mrs. Clarke was preparing in the kitchen?" I looked up from my notes and Clarke was watching me with new interest.

"A cake, a birthday cake for Cheri – that day was her thirteenth birthday."

"Jesus!" The oath was spontaneous. I stared at the floor.

Roger Clarke startled me back to the present. "It was you!"

I didn't know what he was talking about.

"When I got to the hospital yesterday morning, the nurse told me Cheri's uncle had called in the night to check on her. It wasn't her uncle. That was you."

I made no reply.

We sat quiet for a time. Finally, Roger Clarke broke the silence. "The puzzle, the flamingos," he motioned back to Cheri in the kitchen, "it was supposed to be a birthday gift. I didn't buy it. Mary did. I didn't know Cheri liked flamingos. Apparently, she's got a thing for them. I didn't know…" He sat up. "There are more gifts in the closet that I…" He trailed off, looking at a painting at the end of the room, but not seeing it.

I brought him back from wherever he was with another question. "Would Mrs. Clarke have been wearing jewelry when she disappeared?"

"What do you mean?"

"A wedding ring? A watch she always wore? Earrings?"

He nodded. "She always wore her wedding rings. She would have had an emerald on her right hand." He was miming placement of each piece of jewelry as he spoke. "She almost always wore earrings, and she was probably wearing a watch."

"Can you describe the rings?"

He left the room and returned with a pad and a pencil. He worked for about five minutes, then tore off the sheet and handed it to me. He had drawn the rings. The wedding set was not unusual, but the emerald ring was quite distinctive.

"I bought it in Nassau for our tenth anniversary."

At my request, he went to check her jewelry. He couldn't say whether any earrings, chains, or bracelets were missing, but her watch, a gold Piaget, was gone.

I was about to start another line of questioning when young Adam streaked through the room like a frightened mouse. Marsha

Goodwin strode in after him looking totally frustrated. Her appearance could leave little doubt that this was a wealthy woman. She had an are-you-sufficiently-impressed look about her, discordant with chasing after children.

"Hello again, Detective." She turned to Mr. Clarke, "Roger, Adam's teacher talked with me when I picked him up. She said the other kids knew about Mary and said things. He's pretty upset. She suggested keeping him out until Monday."

Roger Clarke shook his head in resignation. "Okay, thanks. And I appreciate you picking him up, Marsha. I'll have other arrangements made by Monday."

"I'm glad I can help. Six?"

"Six sounds good. We'll be there this time."

She smiled and started to leave the room, but I stopped her.

"Ms. Goodwin, did you by any chance see Mary Clarke on the day she disappeared?"

"No. Why?"

"When Mrs. Clarke's body was discovered, she wasn't wearing any jewelry. We're trying to establish what items of jewelry she might have been wearing that day."

"You think that's why she was killed? It was robbery?"

"We don't know why she was killed."

"But that makes sense, doesn't it? Mary had nice jewelry. Didn't she have a beautiful emerald ring?"

"It's missing." Roger said.

"It had to have been robbery."

"Perhaps," I conceded. Her jewelry was certainly missing but I doubted that was why she had been murdered. Not that I had any evidence either way.

After Marsha Goodwin left, I asked Roger Clarke more about his relationship with her. "I don't know much about her. Mary knew her better. We bought this house about three years ago and I think Marsha had already been living in her house for some time before that, years. I know she's divorced. That's really all."

"But she and Mrs. Clarke were close friends."

"I suppose, closer than I realized. Or just nice."

"Meaning?"

"I don't know. When Marsha learned about Mary missing, she stepped in right away. The kids know her and like her, she's been a tremendous help."

Just then, the first crime scene technician arrived and Clarke took the two kids on a dreamed-up errand. Horkheimer showed up soon after and I showed him where I wanted him and his team to concentrate. Then I headed back to the station.

Just as I was wrapping up for the day, Horkheimer called me at my desk. "Hey Frank," he said. "I hoped to catch you. Listen, you need a maid, you could do a lot worse than the one cleaning that house. The bedroom was spotless, the whole place, really. But we did get lucky in the kitchen. High on the side of a cabinet, and on the facing of the outside door, we found just what you were looking for. I thought you would want to know."

I felt my free hand clinch into a spontaneous fist. Horkheimer was telling me the prints in Mary Clarke's kitchen were a match for the prints he had lifted from Greg Devereaux's coffee cup.

7

FRIDAY, EARLY MORNING

A FINGERPRINT ON THE KITCHEN CABINET didn't mean that Devereaux was the murderer. But it did place him at the scene of the crime, which was more than I had on anyone else at this point. And Devereaux had told me that he hadn't been in the house, which was a lie. I didn't have enough to make a case, but I figured he and I ought to have another donut together.

I drove down to Pristine Pools, in time to catch Devereaux there loading his truck. He wasn't happy to see me.

"Good morning, Greg."

"I'm busy, Detective."

"Yes. You. Are." I smirked. "Maybe I should have a talk with your boss about your workload. Some appointments do seem to take you longer than they should, you know. They could fix that."

Hatred flashed in his pale eyes. He came around the truck at me like a gust of hot wind, got close enough that I could tell he had already had breakfast.

"Easy pretty boy! You don't want to assault a police officer."

"What do you want?" he hissed.

"We've gone over this, Greg. The truth, always the truth."

"I told you the truth."

"Bullshit. What did you have going on with Mary Clarke?"

"Nothing."

"What were you doing in her house?"

"I wasn't in her house."

"No?" My voice slipped up an octave where I'm told it has an irritating quality.

"No."

"Your fingerprints are in her house, Greg. You're going to need a new story."

He stepped back and considered me. "You fucking think I'm some dumb jock? You don't have my prints; I've never been arrested."

I told him about his coffee cup's visit to the lab, which took the wind out of his sails. "I want to know," I continued, "what you were doing in Mary Clarke's house. You lie to me again, and I'll call this case solved and arrest you today. Because in case I haven't been clear, you're now the primary suspect in the murder of Mary Clarke."

Without a pause, Greg said again, "I wasn't in her house."

I kept my eyes on his, shaking my head slowly. "Last chance, Greg."

"I don't give a fuck about the prints. I'm telling you, I..." He stopped in mid-sentence, his mouth still open, and his eyes twitched from side to side a couple of times. "Shit." He leaned toward me and smiled. "Yeah. Go fuck yourself, Segal. My prints were inside the kitchen, on the kitchen door." He shook his head side-to-side in mock pity. "Yeah," he said again. "The utility room where the filter is was locked. She couldn't find the key. I went inside with her when she called her husband. Check the phone records."

I knew it was true as soon as he said it. "What phone did she use?"

"The one in the kitchen. Obviously."

"You heard the conversation?"

"Yeah, she just talked to someone, wasn't her husband, found out where the key was and got it for me."

"Where was it?"

"In a kitchen drawer, on a yellow floaty thing, like for a boat key."

I felt deflated and stupid on the way back to the station. I had seen the phone in the kitchen, knew where Horkheimer found the prints. I should have been able to figure out what had likely happened. Devereaux had every right to his anger. I agreed with him.

It was rush hour and the traffic on Kendall Drive was terrible. I remember when the only traffic out this far was the occasional produce truck coming in from the farms down Krome Avenue. The riding stables and open fields that used to line Kendall have been buried under shopping plazas, apartment complexes and planned communities, these last two leaking a constant flow of secretaries, accountants, and armed guards headed to the high-rise offices downtown. I put Devereaux out of my mind and concentrated on working my way through the torrent.

* * *

Someone had cleaned the pot and the coffee was decent. The office already sounded like the newsroom at the *Herald*, but I wasn't hearing it. I was savoring the coffee and turning this case over in my mind. Mary Frances Clarke had been dead for nine days and

I had squat. I worried that the clue I needed might be obvious and I just wasn't seeing it – like that damn kitchen telephone.

"If you're working on another speech for Rolando Ortega, forget it." Wayne dropped into the side chair and rested his left elbow on my desk. He was talking around the ballpoint pen cap in his mouth.

"Because?"

"The guy rolled over. Turns out he had stolen all that stuff and had never told anyone."

"Okay..."

"I mean no one, Stick. Not even a buyer."

"You're kidding!"

"Pretty smart, really. He was worried about getting ripped off or turned in. Says he was planning to make one big sale and then fly back to Bogota the same day."

"And you believe that?"

"I do. We've had the victims in to identify their items. In a couple of cases, we were short things they'd reported missing, but my guess is they padded their insurance claims to cover the deductible."

"And Mary Clarke's murder?"

"Why I'm here, Stick. We put Rolando and a copy of the burglary sheet in the same car and went for a little drive. We'd pull up to houses and he'd tell us yes or no. I added Mary Clarke's address to the list plus a couple of random ones. Ortega said yes only to houses we know he burglarized."

"He's not going to say he'd been in Mary Clarke's house."

Wayne gave me his best slow farmer look and said, "Duh. Of course, he was going to say no either way. He may even be playing us by confessing to burglary in hopes that we will expel him from the country and put him out of reach if evidence does surface. But I don't think so. You were right from the start."

He paused to let me ask what I had been right about, even though he knew I wouldn't.

"It was the car in the driveway. That would have been enough to keep Ortega away."

"Maybe she went out. You said that." He had gotten me into his little game.

"Yeah," he agreed, "I did say that, but I was wrong."

"How do you know?"

"Not about her going out, about it making any difference. It took us an hour to drive by all the places Rolando burglarized, with never a car at any of them. The guy lived in fear of getting caught. He cased his targets for days to be sure they would be empty. Mary Clarke's house had Mary Clarke in it most of the day. No way Rolando Ortega would have tried to enter the Clarke residence." He took the chewed pen cap out of his mouth. "Sorry, but Ortega ain't your murderer."

I had already dismissed Ortega as a serious suspect, but I'd have been happier to be told I was wrong, suspects in this case being as rare as pay increases.

"But," Wayne wasn't through yet, "I still like a burglar for this one. It just has to be a different burglar."

I snorted at the implausibility.

"I'm being serious here. What you need is another burglar in Mary Clarke's neighborhood. And guess what?"

No matter how much I tried to suppress it, I couldn't help but smile. This had all been a shaggy dog story and we were finally going to get to the real punch line. There was only one answer to his question: "There was a burgled house in the Clarkes' neighborhood that Ortega said no to."

The pen cap went back into one side of Wayne's mouth and "there you go" came out of the other side.

Wayne gave me what he had: that the victims' names were Henry and Stacy Walters, that the thief had taken a single item, a diamond and ruby necklace valued at just over $480,000, and that Stacy Walters does not work. He promised to let me know if Property Crimes turned up anything.

After Wayne left, I checked my file for the telephone number of Roberts & Wilson and dialed. The receptionist rang her extension and she answered, "Carmen del Portillo."

"Miss del Portillo, Frank Segal again."

"Good morning, Mr. Segal. Mr. Clarke is not in today."

"Yes, I know. That's okay, I'm calling to talk to you."

"Yes, sir?"

"Sometime last week, did Mrs. Clarke call Mr. Clarke at his office, to ask about a key?"

"Yes sir, she did."

"Do you know what day?"

"It was Tuesday."

"You're sure?"

"Yes, Mr. Clarke was meeting with Mr. Levine when I interrupted to ask him about the key and Mr. Levine's appointment was on Tuesday. Mrs. Clarke couldn't find the key to the pool equipment room," she volunteered.

I thanked her, hung up, and went for a fresh cup of coffee. Then I looked up a florist I had used regularly before the divorce.

I was dispirited by the realization that I hadn't bought flowers in 10 years. I ordered a spray for the funeral and the clerk assured me that it would be there in time for the service.

*   *   *

The funeral was at a Lutheran church in Coral Gables, not far from the offices of Roberts & Wilson. I arrived a half-hour before the service was scheduled to start and took a seat near the back. There were already a few people there.

Marsha Goodwin was the first person to arrive I could identify. She looked distraught and didn't seem to notice me as she went down the aisle, almost to the front of the sanctuary.

Others arrived in twos and threes – friends, neighbors, other parents. A large group arrived with Carmen del Portillo in the middle of it. I also recognized the receptionist from the Roberts & Wilson office and surmised that they had closed the office early to allow everyone to attend the funeral.

Carmen noticed me as she passed and gave me an acknowledging nod. She was dressed entirely in funeral black, but the effect was more stunning than somber. I wondered if she had dressed for Mary or for Roger. I watched her all the way down the aisle, where the entire group from the office, except for Carmen, filed into three pews near the front. Carmen continued to the very front, where she spoke to a man standing near a side door. He nodded and she started back toward her seat, then stopped in front of the closed casket.

The sanctuary door swished open and a tall, thin man in a black suit stood aside and held it. Roger Clarke came through the opening. He had Adam by the hand and Cheri walked at his side. When I looked back at Carmen, she had turned away from the casket, facing Clarke. There was a sadness on her face that only a great painter could capture. Clarke stopped, staring directly at Carmen del Portillo. Or past her at the mahogany casket holding Mary Clarke.

Carmen moved first, slipping back to her seat. The Clarkes continued down the aisle. A couple in their late forties followed, the woman in obvious distress. I guessed her to be Mary Clarke's sister.

The service was emotional, the minister describing Mary Clarke as a devoted wife and mother victimized by an evil beyond our understanding. He didn't dwell there and said a lot to assure everyone that Mary Frances Clarke had gone on to a much better place, a place where fear was unnecessary, a place filled with love, kindness, and consideration – the kinds of qualities she projected during her life on Earth.

My own religion is spotty at best, but I liked the place he was describing. In the unlikely event I ever got there, I would have to make a career change.

I had come to the funeral to observe who attended and had not planned to go to the cemetery. But as the family followed the casket out of the church and I saw tears streaming down Cheri's face, leaving in the middle suddenly felt unacceptable.

At the cemetery, it took a few minutes to get everyone assembled while the sky turned alarmingly black. A late summer afternoon thunderstorm was racing into Dade County from the Everglades. The minister cut his graveside comments short, a blanket of roses was draped over the casket, and workers were soon lowering Mary Clarke's casket into the ground.

First a few big drops fell, then a deluge, as though a bit was spilled from a bucket above our heads just before the whole thing was upended. Nearly everyone sprinted for their cars. The rain slashed under the gravesite awning where the family was seated in folding chairs, and the funeral director urged them into the nearby limousine. The sister and her husband went, taking Adam with them, but neither Roger nor Cheri Clarke appeared to notice the rain. Cheri leaned against her dad, her soaked dress clinging to her small, heaving shoulders. Roger Clarke had his arm around her, his chin on top of her head, and was talking to her very rapidly. I couldn't hear anything he was saying, but I hoped they were the right things.

It also didn't occur to me to leave, but I had stepped to the right, getting a little shelter from the leafy spread of a giant cork tree. When I looked away from the Clarkes, I noticed Carmen del Portillo also in defiance of the elements, standing in the open, right where she had been when the service began. As the rain fell harder, she was more form than substance. She stood motionless, a sculptor's rendering of pathos.

I was looking back toward the gravesite when the blinding flash came, followed immediately by a deafening crack of thunder. The intensity of the light burned the scene into my mind like an old-fashioned flash-powder photograph: the striped awning, the driving rain, the little girl watching the descent of her mother's casket.

I wondered what was going through Roger Clarke's mind.

8

SATURDAY, MORNING

I HAD SATURDAY OFF AND I NEEDED IT. I put the board on top of the car and drove out to Hobie Beach. It was still too early for the crowd and I was afraid it was also too early for the wind, but it looked like there was a decent breeze blowing out in the bay. I rigged the board and headed slowly away from the beach on the zephyrs.

There was a time when Pam and I sailed whenever our days off coincided. We had a 22-foot Catalina and if we had two days, we would be away from the dock at daybreak on day one and not get back to the dock until well after dark on day two. Then we quit sailing together, quit doing much of anything together. I took the boat out a few times alone, but I didn't like it. So, the boat just sat patiently in the driveway until the inevitable divorce.

I sold it to a young couple for less than it was worth because of their excitement over the prospect of owning a boat they could sleep aboard. I told Pam I got more for it than I did and gave her half of the price I made up.

I lost interest in sailing after that. It was something two people did together, something Pam and I did together, and there was no Pam and I. Then, at a beach party, someone showed up with a sailboard. Everyone there tried it, with mostly hilarious results. When my turn came, I stood up on it, lifted the sail out of the water with the boom, and simply took off. It was one-person sailing, pure and uncomplicated, and I was hooked.

On this morning, I worked my way out from behind Key Biscayne, looking for more wind. I concentrated on my form, balancing my weight against the pull of the sail to keep the board driving smoothly across the chop. A pick-up race with another board sailor kept me tweaking sail trim for fractionally more speed. We were neck-and-neck for minutes, each of us earnestly trying to pull ahead of the other, until a huge boat wake spilled her. I tacked and ran back down to where she'd gone in. As I approached, I made a quip about victory, then sat down on my board next to her. She pulled herself up onto her own board and we floated like that, together on the boards in the very middle of the bay, falling into an easy conversation that drifted with us.

Her smile was as bright as her white bikini. She seemed a little younger than me, maybe 40. Red highlights streaked through her dark hair, likely from time in the sun. She was quick and self-assured. Only when she glanced at her watch and announced that she had to go did I realize how long we had been chatting.

"Yeah," I said. "I ought to get back too."

With that she leaped up, tossed a quick goodbye, and accelerated off in the direction of Coconut Grove. I sat on my board and watched her leave, suddenly aware of how good the last hour had been and annoyed at how abruptly it had ended.

She was about one hundred yards away when she kicked the board around, stepped around the mast, and came sailing back. She ripped past me and called out, "Are you single?" She was certainly direct. I liked that.

"Yes," I replied, with an affirmative nod.

She let the sail luff and turned the board around again, facing me. "Me, too. Name's Kelsey. K-E-L-S-E-Y, Cristine Kelsey. I'm in the book. Maybe call me." Then she pulled the sail in, leaned back, and the board took off.

I gave her a double thumbs-up, but she was already past. So, I stood, cupped my hands, and shouted, "Segal!" She looked back. I pointed at myself and shouted again. "Frank Segal!"

She gave an exaggerated nod and I watched her grow smaller before lifting my own sail out of the water and heading the opposite direction, back to where my car was parked.

*   *   *

It was the hottest part of the day and the worst time for it, but I was outside mowing my tiny front lawn shirtless when a small silver Honda came slowly down the street. It turned into my driveway, pulling in too far to be someone just turning around, but I couldn't see who was inside through the dark tinting on the windows.

I wasn't expecting company, but I had some. I stopped the mower, grabbed my shirt from the top of a hedge, and pulled it over my head. Still no movement at the car, so I stood on the lawn and waited. Long seconds passed before the door on the driver's side opened. She stepped out and stood between the door and the car, looking over the top of the car at me. Dark glasses hid her eyes.

I didn't move. I could only guess that she was not sure she wanted to be here and if I approached, she might change her mind and drive away. I waited. She made her decision, stepped back, closed her door, and came around the front of the car. She walked erect, shoulders back, still regal despite wearing floral print jeans and a white blouse.

"Hello, Mr. Segal."

"Miss del Portillo." I smiled at her, but she did not return it.

"I'm sorry about this. I almost didn't get out of my car. I'm still not certain I should be here."

"Well, I am certainly glad you did. It is too hot for that," I nodded toward the silent mower, "and if any of my neighbors have their blinds open, you may well revive their hopes for me."

She managed a faint smile. "I'm glad I can help, but could we talk inside? Is this a good time?" She nodded at the unfinished lawn and I dismissed it with a wave.

I pointed her up the walk then stepped around her to open the door. She smelled so fragrant that I was suddenly quite aware of my own sweaty state.

"Please sit...anywhere you like," I encouraged, turning away to rotate the knob on the wall unit two clicks cooler, then passing through the arched doorway into my kitchen. I returned with two Cokes on ice, setting one on the table in front of her and taking a swig of the other one as I settled into the chair she had not taken. When I crossed my legs, a clump of cut grass fell from my old deck shoes onto the carpet.

"Nice," I mumbled but she was not paying attention.

"I shouldn't have come. They told me it was your day off, but I was afraid I would change my mind if I waited."

"How did you find out where I live?" My number's not listed and I knew that no one at the station would have given her my address.

"The card on the flowers. I got them all so I could manage the thank-you notes for Mr. Clarke. It was nice of you to send flowers."

Efficient and resourceful. And gracious. Sitting in the same room with her, I was having a hard time fitting her into the picture of a murderous conspiracy that had been lurking around in the back of my head since my first visit to Clarke's office.

"They were for Cheri, I think," I said. "I...," but I left the rest unsaid.

She considered me or that for a moment, then gathered herself and pressed forward with what brought her here. "Do the police think Mr. Clarke had something to do with his wife's death?" The question sounded rehearsed and made me wonder if she was here to give information or to get it.

"We're still gathering evidence."

"About anyone other than Roger?"

It was the first time I had ever heard her refer to Clarke by his first name.

"Miss del Portillo, are you romantically involved with Roger Clarke?" She had to have known this would come up, that she would have to explain her actions, yet she still blushed and looked away. I waited.

"Yes."

"It's a motive. A potent motive."

"You're wrong."

"Why? Because you know him? What do you really know about a person in three months? Or did you know Roger Clarke before you went to work at Roberts & Wilson?"

She was startled. "How do you know how long I have been working there?"

"I asked."

"Why?" As soon as the word left her mouth, the look on her face told me she had worked it out. She stood. "I *shouldn't* have come. You're looking in the wrong place, Mr. Segal. I had nothing to do with Mary's death."

"Please sit back down, Miss del Portillo. Please. You're leaping far beyond where we are. I have no reason to suspect you of any involvement beyond catalytic. My inquiry was about Mr. Clarke."

"Roger didn't kill Mary either. He didn't."

"Then help me prove that. Because if he is charged and found guilty, that little boy and that beautiful young girl are going to lose both their parents. You cannot believe that I could find any satisfaction in such a tragic outcome." I was still looking up at her. "You came here to talk with me, Miss del Portillo. There's something you know that you think I should know as well. Please sit down and tell me what that is."

Whatever it was, she still wasn't certain she wanted to share it. "I need for you to tell me something first."

"If I can."

"What if in your investigation you learn that someone..." she was choosing her words carefully, "not the murderer but... someone you talk with, is involved in something illegal. Will that person be arrested?"

"It would depend."

"On what?"

"The nature of the crime. Impact on others. Depth of involvement."

"That's too general."

"It was a general question. Let's try this. I'm a homicide

detective, not a legal crusader. If this someone you are trying to protect is, I don't know, smoking pot, selling underwater lots, cheating on his taxes, not my problem. If he's embezzling funds or smuggling dope, still not my problem, but I'll pass along what I learn to someone who might take an interest. That help any?"

She finally sat back down. "I just don't want to make things worse."

"What is worse than being charged with murder?" I asked. "If you know something that will clearly show Roger Clarke's innocence, you need to tell me."

"Why?" she challenged. "Do you have anything that proves his guilt? No, you don't. If it's Roger's innocence that I'm concerned about, what I should do is just stay out of it. Completely out of it."

I had taken a wrong turn somewhere. I had been anticipating her, expecting her to account for Clarke's whereabouts on the afternoon his wife was murdered. I was sure she was going to hand over a motel receipt or something. Now I was certain that this black-haired beauty knew more than I did about Mary Clarke's death.

"Can you do that? Can you stay out of it?"

"I don't know."

"Someone murdered Mary Clarke, smashed her in the side of the head while she was in the kitchen making a birthday cake for her daughter."

"Dios mio."

She had not known about the birthday.

"If you know something about Mary's murder, how can you even consider hiding it?"

"I'm not hiding anything."

"Ignoring it, then."

She had begun to chew on her lower lip. "I don't know what to do."

"Sure you do. It's why you're here."

"I just don't want to do the wrong thing."

"How can telling me what you know be the wrong thing?"

"Because I don't *know* anything. Something happened that I can only explain one way, but I might be wrong. And if I am and I tell you, I could be causing a lot of trouble for some people."

"Clarke?"

"Yes."

"And if you're right and don't tell me?"

"I know."

She was going to tell me. I sat back in the chair and waited.

"Does the name Herb Steiner mean anything to you?"

"Should it?"

"I don't know. I was just hoping that it might."

"Who is he?"

"He's an ex-client...no, a client of Roberts & Wilson."

"How would I know him?"

"Professionally."

"He's a cop?"

She gave a quick little laugh. "No. I think he's on the other team."

"Herb Steiner?" I shook my head. "It doesn't ring any bells."

She paused a few seconds, then came at me from a different direction. "They are always doing special reports on television about the Mafia in South Florida. Are they accurate?"

"I haven't seen the reports."

"They say that the mob is really active here."

"We have our share of organized crime. So does every major city. What does this have to do with Mary Clarke?"

"The way you found her. Isn't that kind of a Mafia signature?"

"You mean the concrete block?"

"Yes."

I wanted to smile but she was deadly serious. "A cliché," I said. "To sink a body, you have to weigh it down. Anchor, chain, a bag of rocks. A concrete block has the advantages of being easy to get and impossible to identify, but it is no reason to suspect a Mafia link."

"Oh."

"Unless there are other factors. Why do you think this Herb Steiner is involved with the mob?"

"I didn't say that!" she protested.

This time I did smile. "Okay. Do you think Herb Steiner is involved with the mob?"

"I don't know."

"Why don't you tell me what you do know about him?"

She shook her head side to side. "It's not very much."

"Trust yourself, Miss del Portillo. It was enough to get you here."

Her lower lip weathered another assault from her teeth. "Do you know what Roberts & Wilson does?"

"It's an investment firm."

"Financial planners. Not just stocks and bonds, but insurance, tax shelters, individual retirement programs. Tangible investments like art, gems, precious metals, rare coins."

"Okay."

"The clients are very wealthy. Company and client relationships are normally close and long-term. Confidentiality is paramount, of course. That's why..."

She stopped and I acknowledged with a nod.

"It's my job to be discreet." She trailed off and I wasn't sure she would continue. Then she did. "But something happened about three weeks ago. I don't know what it was, but it was a big problem. Mr. Clarke got all the officers together in his office and I could hear him shouting right through the wall. He fired two of the officers that day, and a day later he fired a third one."

"He owns the company?" I asked.

"I think so. Anyway, after the meeting, he called me in and dictated a letter to one of Chip Harris' clients. Mr. Harris was one of the officers fired. The letter just said that due to company policy, we would no longer be able to service the account. The account was a company called Latin-American Cleaners. Herb Steiner was the client; he owns Latin-American Cleaners.

"Two days later two men came to the office to meet with Mr. Clarke, hard-looking men – like boxers dressed up in suits. After about five minutes in the office, he ordered them out. He was quite upset."

"They were there about the Steiner account?"

"Yes. I'm sorry this is such a long story, but the rest of it won't make sense without the first part."

"You tell it your way," I reassured her. Her untouched drink had turned clear on top, dark at the bottom. "Let me get you something fresh to drink."

She waved me off. "After that, Mr. Steiner called Mr. Clarke a couple of times, but their conversations were quite short. He stopped calling. Monday was the day that you came to the office and told Mr. Clarke about finding Mary. He left after that and I didn't expect to see him in the office for at least the rest of the week. But Tuesday morning he came in, wanting to be occupied maybe. About nine, he got a telephone call which I put through."

She paused and looked away from me, evaluating it one more time I supposed, before she gave it all to me. It must have come out the same way again. When she looked back, her black eyes were glistening. "At first, when the door flew open, I thought that the call must not have gone through. But he came out of his office in a full run. I hardly recognized him; his face was so distorted. About halfway down the hall he suddenly stopped, ran back to my desk and grabbed my telephone. The dial was upside-down to him, and he couldn't have dialed it anyway in his state, but he tried.

"I had no idea what was going on. Each time he failed to dial the number he wanted, he got more frantic. Finally, I grabbed his hand to stop him and said, 'Let me.' I don't think he even knew who I was. When I asked him who he was trying to call, he said 'home.'" She imitated his response in a hoarse whisper.

"I dialed the number for him. A neighbor was staying with the kids and she answered. Roger wanted to know if Cheri was there. He made the lady go check. He was so strange…I just didn't know what to think. The lady must have confirmed that Cheri was there and then he just turned and left.

"About two hours later he called me from home, sounding calm. He apologized for the frenzy and tried to reassure me that everything was okay, that he was just upset over Mary's death and should not have come into the office. Then he told me that he was expecting a hand-delivered package that afternoon and he wanted me to put it into our vault. He said it like it was an afterthought, but it was the real reason he called.

"The package came like he said, but the man delivering it was one of the boxers Roger had ordered to leave. It wasn't until then that I made a connection between the telephone call that morning and what followed. The caller was Mr. Steiner.

"You have to understand, I had never seen Roger like that. It frightened me. I knew I needed to know what was in that package, so I opened an end of it. It was full of money, cash, a lot of cash!"

9

SUNDAY, MORNING

CARMEN DEL PORTILLO HAD STAYED in my living room for another hour on Saturday, filling in the details of her story, worrying that her indiscretion was getting Clarke in trouble or putting him in danger. I think she also worried that talking to me would end her relationship with him. Yet there she'd been, taking those risks to do the "right" thing. I felt a growing admiration.

I had tried to assure her that I would move cautiously until I knew what I was dealing with. The truth was that I had no idea if her information had anything to do with Mary Clarke's death. Nor did anything she'd told me relieve Clarke of my suspicions, but I didn't tell her that.

Roger Clarke could fill in the blanks, but because he wasn't sharing any details with the secretary sharing his bed, I didn't think he was going to be eager to discuss any of it with me. I decided to find out what I could about Herb Steiner before I went to see Clarke.

I spent the morning in Vice. They'd never heard of Herb Steiner, but one of the guys knew about Latin-American Cleaners, he had his suits cleaned there. The yellow pages listed a half-dozen locations for the small dry-cleaning chain.

*   *   *

When I called the Clarke house, Cheri answered.

"Hello, Cheri, this is Detective Segal."

"Oh, hi, Mr. Segal, I'll get my dad."

"How's the puzzle coming?"

"I haven't worked on it much."

I didn't like the way she sounded. Clarke came on the line and I told him that I needed to talk with him. He tried to put me off, but I didn't give him a choice. We agreed that I would come by at 3:00.

Carmen del Portillo had given me something that showed promise and I'd been turning the case over in my mind. As I cruised down Old Cutler Road toward the Clarkes' neighborhood, it occurred to me that if someone gave me a house like Roger Clarke's, I would have to move. My income couldn't pay the property taxes. Where had all that money come from? He could have made it all legally. Despite my tendency to suspect otherwise, I knew very well that much of Dade County's wealth is perfectly legitimate. But there is tainted money in Miami as well. Was Clarke the innocent victim Carmen had portrayed him to be, or was he somehow caught up in his own web?

When the boats docked in Snapper Creek flashed by, I realized that I had been lost in thought and passed 105th Street. I turned around and went back.

Clarke opened the door before I could ring the bell. He led me down the hall, past the closed door of Cheri's room, and to a door at the very end. Opening it, he waved me through. I felt a slight twinge of envy; this was his space. An oriental desk with elaborate inlay sat in front of an entire wall of teak bookcases. In one corner was a blue porcelain vase, at least four feet tall, decorated with a parade of intensely colorful peacocks. In the opposite corner was a lighted world globe in a brass stand. Beside the door a leather sofa and two leather chairs gathered around a brass table.

I took one of the chairs and he went over to a pair of louvered cabinet doors next to a built-in aquarium. Folding them open, he revealed a wet bar.

"Drink?"

"No, thanks."

He decided not to drink alone and came across the room to the couch. When the leather quit chirping, he asked me why I'd come.

"How is Cheri?" I was not yet ready.

"Okay."

"It seemed like she took the funeral really hard."

"She was close to her mother. You were at the funeral?"

I nodded. "Couldn't have just been a sunny day with birds singing."

"At the cemetery, too?"

I gave a nod.

"Why? Because whoever killed her might show up?"

"Maybe the killer was there. It's a reason to attend a victim's funeral."

"It seems disrespectful."

"I did not intend any disrespect. And I had other reasons."

"Cheri?"

"She's one."

He raised his eyebrows, inviting me to go on. I paused, realizing that if Mary Clarke's murder was connected to the information Carmen del Portillo had shared with me, I needed Roger Clarke's full commitment. I thought I saw a way.

"I was there for the same reasons I'm a cop."

His high forehead wrinkled a bit, but he was silent.

"Because I care. Because I know the difference between right and wrong." I stopped and looked at him, hard, doing my best to show contempt. "Because someone killed Mary Clarke and it matters to me," I baited.

"You don't think it matters to me?"

"Does it? Does it really matter? Sure, you care. She was the mother of your children and her death will forever scar their lives, especially Cheri, given her age, given her obvious attachment to her mother. Christ, her birthday is going to remind her of her mother's murder for the rest of her days. But for you there's a bright side. The fire has gone out in your marriage and when this is all over, you're going to be free to spend more time where there is fire. That's got to lighten the burden, right?"

His face had gone completely red, but he was in control. He stood. "We're done here." His voice was measured, and caustic.

"Oh, you think I'm out of line." I remained seated, looking up at him, my disdain obvious in my posture and my voice. "Really? Surely you don't think no one knows about you and your secretary?"

"Get. Out. Now."

"Here's the thing, Clarke. If it had been the bloated body of Carmen del Portillo that we dragged up on shore, you would be demanding that we find her killer, not ordering me out of your house. This was Mary's house, too. How about you find the same outrage for her? Why don't you start by telling me who killed her?"

"What?"

"Was it Herb Steiner?"

That stopped him cold.

"You can help me or not, but if you don't, when I have Mary's killer locked up, I will document every financial indiscretion I came across and drop that package on Vice. Do you understand what I am telling you?"

He was still stunned. "Wh…how do you know about Herb Steiner?"

"I want to know more. Sit down, tell me about him. This is what help looks like, Mr. Clarke."

"I can't." It was a whisper.

"Did he tell you that Cheri would be next?"

His eyes widened. "You have my phone tapped!"

I stayed quiet, allowing the blank face I'd been perfecting for 20 years to say whatever he wanted it to say.

He wilted back into his chair and dropped his forehead into the palm of his hand. "Oh, God."

He was physically a big man, but this was the second time I had seen him fold under pressure. Sitting there in his designer pullover and his $90 slacks, he had no idea what to do now.

"Maybe a drink wouldn't be a bad idea," I suggested. I didn't want a drink, but I also didn't want him to freeze up. He stood and walked mechanically back to the bar. "Gin and tonic – light," I said over my shoulder.

I heard a muffled thump as a glass hit the carpet behind me. When I looked around, he was standing with both hands on the bar, staring down at the fallen glass. I turned back and waited. It was quiet for a moment, just the sound of the gentle bubbling of the aquarium filter, but eventually I heard the clink of glassware, the sound of pouring, the rasp of a screw cap.

When he was re-seated with the drink in his hand, I asked him again about Herb Steiner.

"I've never met him. I don't really know anything about him."

"Chip Harris has met him."

"Jesus. If you already have it all, why are you talking with me?"

Carmen had done well.

"I want to know how you're involved. I don't have it all, but all is exactly what I want. Don't leave anything out."

"Involved? Yeah, I'm involved." He repositioned himself on the sofa, touched the drink to his lips, then cradled the glass in both hands. "But I didn't know that until last month. The bastards tied a block to my company, too. Twenty years."

"What happened last month?"

"Our annual audit. It revealed that we had failed to show large cash transactions that by law we are required to report. One of our officers..."

"Chip Harris."

"Jesus, yes."

"How much money?"

"Close to four million dollars."

"All of it from Herb Steiner?"

"Yes."

Clarke claimed to not know about the transactions before the audit. He said that as soon as he found out, he took steps to correct the situation. I didn't know the truth about what he knew before the audit, but I did know that the steps he took after were a cover-up. He had fired Harris and two other officers Harris implicated. He had attempted to sever his relationship with Steiner and then it was supposed to be business as usual. Except that he had not considered what kind of person Steiner might turn out to be.

"You called Steiner?"

"Yes. And a couple of days later two men, his men, showed up at the office. They made threats, implied threats. I showed them the door.

"Then Steiner himself called, a couple of times. The first time he came across real smooth, as though this were nothing more than a little misunderstanding that we could resolve. I made it clear that we didn't want his business."

"Made it clear how?"

"It was clear."

"But he called again."

"Yeah, the second time to try threatening. He told me that if I didn't reconsider, if I didn't keep him as a client…he said I would be 'making a very dangerous mistake.' Those were his words."

"What did you do?"

"I told him that I was 'reconsidering,' that I was thinking about turning the whole matter over to the police."

"You think the money was illegal?"

"Of course it was illegal! That kind of cash from dry cleaning?"

"Steiner has a chain of stores, right? It's a cash business."

"Not that much cash. And Chip was hiding it for him. No, it's dirty, probably drugs."

"Is Harris a user?" I asked.

"A what?"

"Drugs, was Harris using drugs? That his connection to Steiner?"

"I...I don't know."

"Take a guess. Harris is the guy who put you here."

"Cocaine."

I nodded.

"I talked with him, a couple of times, told him it had to stop. He worked for me for 14 years, and it was party stuff, not like he needed treatment or..."

"Where's the money now, from the account? You closed the account, sent Steiner a check?"

"He doesn't have an account, never has. Chip was buying coins: Krugerrands, Eagles, whatever was available, and delivering them back to Steiner."

"With which he could open a legitimate account in another investment or brokerage firm?"

"He could do anything with them. It's ironic, isn't it? We were the ones really in the laundry business, not Steiner."

"If he didn't have an account, how did an audit expose it?"

"The hard-asset purchases. Not being associated with an account caught the auditor's attention."

"When did he call again?"

"Steiner?"

"Yeah."

"Last Tuesday, morning."

"He called you?"

"Yes."

"At your office?"

"Yeah."

"What did he say?"

"You already know."

"Humor me."

"That a package would be delivered at two, that if I didn't handle it as always, my daughter would be next." He choked up a little on the last bit.

"'Your daughter will be next.' Like that? Not, 'We will kill your daughter next,' or 'If your wife wasn't enough, we can do your daughter next?'"

He closed his eyes to replay that telephone conversation. "'A package will be delivered to your office this afternoon at two. Handle it as always or your daughter will be next.' Just like that."

"Okay, good. What did you do?"

"I called home. Then I came home."

"To be sure Cheri was all right?"

"Yes."

"And then," I said, cocking my head, "you reopened your laundry business."

"What was I going to do?" He was angry again. "You, you're here because Mary is already dead. You going to keep the same thing from happening to Cheri? I don't think so. But I can. And why not? Someone is going to handle the damn transactions for them. Why not me?"

"And what, just forget about Mary? No, worse than that, you're going to make her killer a partner in your business. The controlling partner, it sounds like."

He opened his mouth to protest, but nothing came out.

"You're in this, Clarke, and you better pull yourself together. There is only one cure for a malignancy."

I'm not much of a believer in divine intervention, but the hesitant knock on the door at that moment was close. When Clarke acknowledged it, Cheri came into the room with Adam in tow. She said hello to me and then turned her attention to her dad. She needed money to buy a pair of shoes for Adam. From the conversation, I gathered that Mary's sister was staying for a few days to help. She would be driving, but it was clearly Cheri who was in charge.

After she left, Clarke sighed, "After the funeral, she came home crying and stayed in her room all night. Saturday morning was a new day. She got up and started straightening up the house, watering the plants; she made a grocery list..." He trailed off.

"She's doing what she thinks she has to do. She'll expect no less from you."

10

MONDAY, MORNING

IN A MEETING WITH A COUPLE OF GUYS from Vice, I gave them everything I had, everything both Carmen del Portillo and Roger Clarke had given me on Herb Steiner. Because no one had seen Herb Steiner, I couldn't give them much to go on. We bounced it around for a while, but all we really knew, suspected, was that someone was delivering cash to Roberts & Wilson for the purchase of gold and other hard assets.

We didn't know who that person was, only that he identified himself as Herb Steiner. We didn't know where the money came from, only that it was cash and Mr. Steiner didn't want the government to know about it. Nor did we know that Steiner had anything to do with Mary Clarke's death, the only connection being Roger Clarke's claim of an implied confession.

The pieces did seem to fit together, with nothing Clarke had finally given up contradicting anything that Carmen had told me, but I felt unsettled. I still could not rule out what Carmen feared, that this business with Steiner had nothing to do with Mary Clarke's death. Was Clarke clever enough to be using it to shift suspicion about his wife's death away from himself? Could I be underestimating him? Might he even have planned this from the start, setting himself up to be victimized by the mob? Hadn't he mentioned the Mafia in our first conversation? I didn't think anything of it then, but it seemed curious now.

I also had to keep the possibility open that Carmen del Portillo might be directly involved, that her story was a carefully crafted decoy. If so, her delivery had been so masterful that for now I believed in the authenticity of the instilled values that seemed to define her.

Clarke didn't live on such a high plane, so I was not yet ready to discount him.

My meeting with Vice concluded with them opting to remain on the sidelines until the murder investigation ended. Aside from the risks of conflict, the clearer picture that was sure to emerge from the murder investigation would provide them with a better starting point. That course was fine with me.

From Vice I went to see my lieutenant, to let him know what I had in mind. I anticipated his reaction and knew it would be a hard sell.

"You want to put a…what, a financial adviser in the hot seat, alone with a bad guy we don't have a profile on and who you think might be connected?"

When he summarized it like that, I had second thoughts, but pressed forward anyway, arguing that this would not represent a significant increase in danger for Roger Clarke and that he was insistent that we do it. The lieutenant ultimately agreed, but I knew how thin the ice he was letting me out onto was.

*   *   *

The sun on the white concrete was blinding as I came out of the cool shade of the parking garage. At the first intersection, a black Trans-Am sped across in front of me, well after his light had changed to red. What I had told Carmen about not being a legal crusader was not entirely true. I wanted to chase the prick down and write him up, make his already outrageous insurance premiums astronomical. We all have to live here together and we damn sure better respect each other's rights. That's what laws are about, what cops are about. We can't let you barrel through a red just because you're in a hurry. Or burglarize a house just because you need the money. Or drop a young mother off a bridge just because...

Because what? Why had Mary Clarke been killed? A man shoots another in an argument, we know why. An abused wife stabs her husband in his sleep, we get it. A son blows up his wealthy mother, a man strangles his wife's lover, a buyer is machine-gunned in a drug deal, a bank robber kills an armed guard, the acts might be unfathomable but the why isn't. Even when a crazed junkie executes an elderly convenience store clerk with a bullet to the back of the head, drugs are the why.

But why Mary Clarke...alone...in her own kitchen...in the middle of the day...making a birthday cake for her daughter? If Clarke was telling the truth, then the smart money had to be on Herb Steiner. I was having difficulty with what a drastic step that was just to keep someone laundering his money, although I was aware there are some in the drug business who except for walking on two legs exhibit not a single other human characteristic.

And if Clarke wasn't telling the truth? I was sure that Roger and Mary had not been holding hands and gazing deeply into each other's eyes for some time, but what would make murder preferable to divorce? Child custody maybe? Or money? Mary would be entitled to half of their assets. Did that mean the business, too? Carmen thought Clarke owned the business. Whatever his stake, if he lost half of it, would that cost him control of the company? He had acted more concerned about what Steiner was doing to his company than what had happened to his wife. Maybe this was all about money.

I was so caught up in these thoughts that I found myself pulling into a parking space across the street from the Roberts & Wilson offices without any recollection of driving there. I wondered if I had run any red lights.

Before I got out of the car, I gave Pool Boy Devereaux the once over. He was the only one I could place at the scene. Maybe he did have something going with Mary Clarke. Or he wanted to and she refused, so he raped her. The ME's report didn't say that she wasn't raped, just that there was no evidence of rape. Which summed up what I had on Devereaux, no evidence.

I ruled out Rolando Ortega too, but there was Wayne Thomas' theory about one of Ortega's colleagues, the unidentified burglar. Stranger things have happened.

Carmen del Portillo came to the reception area to escort me back to Roger Clarke's office. As soon as the hallway turned, she stopped me with her hand on my sleeve.

"His telephone is bugged?"

I shrugged and showed my upturned palms.

She looked puzzled, then not. Her shoulders sagged just a bit as she exhaled. It was a breath she had been holding since Saturday, waiting for Roger to find out about her betrayal.

"Thank you."

He didn't deserve her. Donnie Watson didn't deserve Beth

Crawford either when she decided to break up with me in high school. But they're still married, and one of their six kids is my godchild.

"He may still find out," I warned.

She nodded.

"How is he?"

"Determined."

When we got to Clarke's office, what I observed was more than determination. He was angry. A hard, cold anger. A dangerous anger. I wondered if I would be able to trust his judgment. It was the second time in an hour that I was having second thoughts.

I had outlined on Sunday what we needed to do. His eyes were red and puffy and I wondered if he had been awake all night thinking about it.

"No," he said. "I drove to Tampa and back last night. Tarpon Springs."

When I looked blank, he went on. "I took Adam and Cheri up there to stay with some dear friends."

"Mary's sister…?"

"Yeah. She wanted to take them home with her, but I was afraid they would be too easy to find there. She has a flight home this morning, eleven forty-five." He glanced at his watch. "That leaves me as the only Clarke in town."

"That's good." His judgment seemed sound so far. "What about Carmen? Did Chip Harris know about the relationship?"

He actually flinched. He had not thought about the risk to her. "I…shit, I didn't think so, but you know."

I held up my hand. "Easy. No reason to think she is in danger, no more than any other member of your staff. Let's treat her that way."

He gave a reluctant nod, then moved on to what he had been thinking about. "I may know how to get him here."

That was the part I was having trouble with, so I told him to go on.

"Drug businesses," he said, "they're run like any other business, right?"

I thought the question was rhetorical, then realized he was waiting for my response. "How do you mean?"

"Maximize profits, minimize expenses."

"No, no, not like that. They use a million-dollar airplane once, then abandon it, or sink a hundred-foot freighter after off-loading the cargo. Profits are so enormous that expenses hardly matter."

"So, if I decided to charge Steiner, say, half for laundering his money, that wouldn't get a reaction?"

"No, that would get a reaction. It might get your funeral."

"But you just said…"

"Legitimate expenses. If they think you're trying to screw them, they won't ignore that."

"Couldn't I just be driving a harder bargain for a risk he knows I don't want to take?"

I could see where he was going with this. "He'll never buy it. He killed your wife and threatened your daughter. You will do it for nothing if he tells you to. Steiner is never going to negotiate with you."

He sat back in defeat. "Then what?"

"I don't know. Maybe he needs to come here to instruct you… to straighten something out. But he has to think he initiated the visit, not that you want him here."

"Wouldn't he just send one of his thugs for that?"

"Yeah, probably." I was getting a headache.

His telephone buzzed and he got up to answer it. He said, "Yes," and hung up.

"What if..." I started, but he stopped me.

The office door opened and Carmen came in with a tray, which she placed on the table between us without a comment and went quickly back out the door. The scent of her perfume, the same one she had worn on Saturday, was soon displaced by the pungent aroma of fresh coffee.

Clarke lifted the thermal pot and filled the two cups. "I don't want her to know much about all of this."

I was silent.

"You were about to say?"

"They made the delivery last week, right?"

"The cash? Yes."

"Have you processed it?"

"You mean purchased gold? No. This is my first day in the office since Steiner called."

"Is there a way to screw up the transaction so badly that Steiner himself will want to come in to school you? Or chastise you?"

He shook his head. "The purchase of gold is straightforward."

"What if you invested it in something else?"

"We wouldn't..."

"Harris is gone." I interrupted.

"Right." He sat motionless for a time, working his way through it. The room was so quiet that I became aware of the buzzing of one of the fluorescent tubes overhead and the popping of the glass wall as it reacted to refrigerated air on one side and the hot Florida sun on the other.

"I wonder...," he said, then stood and left the office. I was still looking outside, watching an Eastern DC-9 drop into Miami International in the distance when he came back. He had a file with him.

"Steiner never signed a power of attorney form."

"Why would he want to give you power of attorney?"

"He wouldn't. And for gold purchases, we wouldn't need it. But if we screwed up and bought securities in his name, we couldn't sell them, we couldn't undo the transaction, unless we had a limited power of attorney on file. Or unless he came in and signed the sale order."

"Bingo."

The number in Chip Harris' Steiner file was for an answering service, but Steiner called back in less than 10 minutes.

Roger Clarke turned out to be such a great actor that I found myself even more concerned than before about his own involvement in his wife's death. He was pleading, almost crying on the telephone, and carrying on in such a disjointed way that Steiner must have had difficulty in understanding exactly what Clarke was telling him. When Steiner finally figured it out, he was clearly furious.

"I know. I know. I didn't know." Clarke was saying. "Please don't hurt my kids. It wasn't my fault – I mean it was my fault. It was a mistake. Bill didn't..."

I could hear Steiner yelling again. Clarke waited until he was through.

"We can fix it. It's not a problem. We can get most of the

money back. We can get *all* of the money back. It's no problem. Really. It's just that...it might be...uh...it might be a little bit of an inconvenience. I don't know what else...."

I couldn't hear Steiner now, but then Clarke said, "The certificates are in your name."

Steiner was screaming out of the receiver again.

"I know. I know. It was stupid," Clarke agreed. "I'm sorry. We'll fix it, just don't hurt my kids. Please. Please...." His voice just faded out.

There was a lull before Steiner must have said something.

"You have to sign them," Clarke said quietly.

Steiner was audible again.

"You're right," Clarke agreed again. "It'll take just a minute, and that's it. It won't ever happen again. We can do it this afternoon...no...I must get them here. Tomorrow, whenever you say."

Clarke listened, then said, "OK. It will just take...," but he did not finish the sentence because Steiner was gone. After putting the receiver back in its cradle, he looked up at me with a big smile, the first I had seen on Roger Clarke. "Herb Steiner will be here at eleven tomorrow morning."

11

TUESDAY, EARLY MORNING

I PICKED ROGER CLARKE UP at his house at 6:00 a.m. He looked like he still hadn't slept. As we headed toward the station, I again began having second thoughts about how this might go down. Maybe second thoughts were what had kept Clarke awake all night.

"You can back out if you want to. Nobody in the department really wants you to do this anyway."

"I'm not backing out!"

"We can just pick him up when he comes in. Since we don't know who he really is, he may be someone we're already after."

"And maybe not. Either way, not for Mary's murder."

"No, not for Mary's murder."

"Then I'm not backing out."

An assistant from the State Attorney's office met us in a conference room on the third floor. She was an ASA I hadn't worked with before. She introduced herself as Cricket Nixon. I wondered if that name was a harbinger or a handicap.

It was neither. Cricket Nixon was good. For more than 45 minutes she instructed Clarke on what he could and could not say. She ran through a half-dozen examples of entrapment and showed him how to get the same statement without corrupting the evidence. Clarke listened and answered all the questions right, but he was intensely critical of all the concern over violating Steiner's rights.

"It's the system we have," Ms. Nixon explained. "Until someone officially changes the rules, they're the ones we have to play by."

"And even if he says: 'My name is Herb Steiner and I murdered your wife,'" Clarke said, "he still might get off."

She looked over at me and I gave her a shrug. "He might. But it will be harder for him to go free if we have a confession like that."

Clarke shook his head. "If he has enough money, he'll never spend a day in jail, and you know it. And I know he has enough money."

"Every corrections facility in the state is packed like a sardine can," I said. "People go to jail."

"Poor people," he said. "Blacks. Not Herb Steiner."

Ms. Nixon was Black and went conspicuously silent.

"Wow," I said. "Then why are you here, Mr. Clarke?"

"Because this bastard killed my wife," he blurted, then regained control and added, "You said it: I'm in this, no matter what. So, I have to do this. I need to do it. And who knows, maybe something will come of it."

After Ms. Nixon left, a technician showed up to fit Clarke with the wire. We decided on a tiny transmitter taped to Clarke's chest beneath his shirt. I would be in an adjacent office with the receiver, monitoring and recording the conversation.

*　　*　　*

At 9:00 a.m. I had Roger Clarke back in his office. I set myself up in an office vacated by one of the recently fired officers. It had a clear view of Carmen's desk and the waiting area, and I could also see the door to Clarke's office.

As Clarke and Carmen discussed current office issues, I checked my end of the bug. Through the tiny earphone I could hear them both clearly. I stopped the recorder and played it back to confirm it was working.

I stayed at my post for almost two hours, but I couldn't risk Steiner showing up early with me not there. I busied myself at the desk, trying to look like a purveyor of wise investments, but as the real officers whizzed by the door in their English suits and Italian shoes, I realized that fiction would not stand up to close observation. I was as inconspicuous as Orphan Annie at the Queen's Gala. I hoped Steiner would be focused on his errand.

At 10:50, Carmen buzzed me to let me know that Herb Steiner was in the lobby. While she went to get him, I called Roger Clarke. He said he was ready, but he sounded tense, frightened maybe. "We can still abort," I said.

"No. You were right about him, and about me. It's time both were corrected." He hung up without giving me a chance to reply. I felt as if he had just dragged his fingernails across a blackboard.

I had no time to give it additional thought because Carmen returned with two men a step behind her. The guy in the brown suit had a narrow face, a beak of a nose, and curly black hair in full revolt. He couldn't have been more than five feet five inches tall. I figured he was Steiner because I recognized the other guy. The one in pinstripes was Jack Boggs, and he had a rap sheet as long as the Sweetwater telephone book. He was a strong arm for Arturo Ribera.

If you dropped Arturo Ribera into an open cesspool, he

would foul it. If Steiner was fronting for Ribera, Clarke was involved with the devil, himself. Suddenly I didn't like this plan at all. The stakes had gotten too high. I pushed myself away from the desk, but before I could get out of the chair Carmen was already past, leading Steiner into Clarke's office, with Boggs veering away to take a seat in the waiting area. I rolled my knees back under the desk, pushed the earphone into my right ear and punched the record button.

"...sit down." It was Clarke's voice all right, but with a hard edge I'd not heard before.

"Let's get this over with." Steiner's accent was New York maybe New Jersey. He spoke rapidly, clipped, impatient.

"Were you at the funeral? The police told me that the murderer sometimes shows up at the funeral." Clarke's approach was hostile. This wasn't the way we had discussed it. I hoped this thing wasn't already off the rails, that Clarke was just reacting to something he had noticed.

"What funeral?"

"The one for my wife."

"Your wife died? Gosh, I'm really sorry to hear about that."

Clarke began to laugh, a harsh, ugly laugh. "I can't believe this. Look at you, a fucking sideshow freak. A fucking midget You sound like a real person on the telephone."

"Have a good time, Clarke, but don't go too far," Steiner said

I was thinking the same thing.

"Or what? You ever look in a mirror? You think I'm intimidated by a little weasel like you? The part I can't figure out is who would trust you with so much cash. It doesn't matter because as soon as I throw your low-slung butt out of here, you're going to have to crawl back and tell them that you lost it. Then I'll be at your funeral."

"The papers, Clarke. Now."

Clarke laughed again. "Your scam's over."

"My scam? I'm telling you…"

"You've never been inside my house. A worm like you doesn't have the balls to walk into someone's house in broad daylight. If you had, the smell would still be there. So, as it turns out, I won't be needing your signature. In fact, I think you're in the wrong office. We have no records of us ever handling any investments for you. Ever."

"What the fuck's wrong with you? You looking for another funeral?"

"Am I putting you in that much danger, Herbie? Cause that can't be a threat aimed at me. You know as well as I do that you never had anything to do with my wife's death."

"You know, Clarke, you're kinda right. It was really you that killed her." That staccato New Jersey voice was getting louder in my ear. I guessed that Steiner was leaning across the desk, into Roger Clarke's face. "I just helped her over the bridge railing. And I'm only going to tell you one last time, you're about to kill your daughter the same way. Get me the fucking papers."

That was enough. We had him. For the second time my pants cleared the chair seat, and for the second time I sat back down. The earphone was making a strange sound and my mind was frantic to make sense of it. It was a rasping sound with an occasional thump. Then Clarke said, "What the hell you think you're doing?" followed by a tearing sound.

At the same instant that the sounds made sense to me, Steiner said, "You son of a bi..." and the bug went dead. I was around the desk and to the doorway when the quiet of the office was shattered by a gunshot. A gallon of acid hit the pit of my stomach. Carmen screamed and stood up. Behind her, Jack Boggs jumped up, pulled a gun from somewhere inside his coat, and charged toward the door to Clarke's office.

I dropped to a crouch with my own gun in both hands and screamed, "Hold it Boggs! Police! Drop the weapon!"

Carmen dove to her right, away from the deadly line between Boggs and me. I had pressure on the trigger, ready to drop him if he brought the gun around.

Instead, he froze, never looked my way, and held both hands out from his body.

"Put the gun down."

He obeyed.

"Now back away from it." I was watching Boggs and watching the door to Clarke's office at the same time. A lot of the employees had come running when the shot went off. I waved my gun for effect: "Everybody out of sight! Now!" They disappeared.

"Carmen, stay down. Is there another way out of Roger's office?"

"Yes."

"Through the restroom?" My eyes were still on Boggs.

"Yes. It opens into a conference room and you can get out to the elevators that way."

"Damn it! Goddamn it! Stay down, but if you can reach your phone, call nine-one-one. Tell them an officer needs assistance. Get an ambulance, too." I heard her squeak and start to cry, but she pulled the phone off her desk and made the call.

"Face down, Boggs! Now!"

I crossed the room in a crouch and picked up his gun, clicking on the safety and shoving it under my waistband. Then with the barrel of my gun to his neck, I cuffed Boggs' hands behind his back. "Don't move, not even a twitch."

The door to Roger Clarke's office was still closed. I crouched against the wall next to the door and listened. Nothing. That lightning-seared image of Cheri at the cemetery flashed through my mind. A wave of nausea swept over me. "Carmen, get out of here. Now!" I heard the rustle as she scrambled toward the hallway.

With my left hand, I reached up and slowly turned the knob. One breath. Two breaths. Three deep breaths. A quick look at Boggs and I pushed the door hard. It swung all the way open and...nothing but silence. One more breath and I swung into the doorway with my gun leveled.

Clarke was there, still sitting in his big leather chair, only his necktie covering his bare chest where the wire had been. He gave me a crooked smile and relaxed his right hand. A pistol fell onto the top of the desk with a thud.

Steiner was still there, too, staring eye level at the soles of my shoes. There was a hole in the center of his forehead. A chunk of the back of his head was lying next to a potted peace lily.

12

TUESDAY, MIDDAY

THE CORAL GABLES POLICE SWARMED all over the Roberts & Wilson offices. Emergency had also arrived, but after looking at the damage inflicted by the hollow point .357 at point-blank range, they found chairs to wait in until we were through with the body.

Roger Clarke was in one of the other offices being sick. Carmen del Portillo was in there with him, looking less rattled than I'd have imagined. At one point, she came out of the room to request help from the paramedics, asking whether they could do something for Clarke.

Harry Freeman was the Coral Gables detective who caught the case. I didn't touch anything until he arrived. I didn't want to be the cause of a flare-up between Metro and the Gables. Freeman turned out to be easygoing and glad to have me on the scene. The only thing missing from the office when Freeman arrived was Roger Clarke. Clarke's .357 was still on the desk. In Steiner's left hand was the bug Clarke had been wearing. Under the desk, near Steiner's right hand, was a .32 automatic. Freeman lifted Steiner's coat and found the empty holster. He slipped the pistol into it. It was a custom fit.

After Freeman was satisfied with his examination of the crime scene, we went into the office where I had been monitoring the conversation between Steiner and Clarke. I gave him a quick overview of what had preceded their meeting, then let him listen to the tape.

"Steiner found the wire?"

"That's what it sounds like," I agreed.

"What did Clarke say?"

"I haven't talked with him. I figured you would like to have him first."

"Did you know he had a gun?"

"No. When I heard the shot, I was sure that Clarke was the victim."

"Lucky for him he had a gun. For you, too, I guess. My lieutenant wouldn't like it at all if I let a civilian get killed during a set-up."

"Mine isn't going to care much for it this way either, but you're right; it would have been worse the other way."

"What do you have on this Steiner character?"

"Not much. But the other guy," I pointed to Boggs, still cuffed but up in a chair, "used to work for Arturo Ribera. His name's Jack Boggs."

Freeman was scribbling everything in his notebook. "You think this Steiner is connected to Ribera?"

"I don't know."

Freeman listened to the tape again. I told him that I would send him a copy.

At Freeman's suggestion I went with him to talk to Roger Clarke. The office Clarke was in still had a brass plaque on the door that read Chip Harris, Vice-President. When Chip read in the paper about a shooting at his old place of business, I wondered if he would put it together with Mary Clarke's death. I hoped so, but if not, I was now sure that Vice would explain it all to him when the time came.

We found Clarke lying on a sofa with a half-dozen damp paper towels across his face. Carmen was gone.

"Mr. Clarke, we need to talk to you for a few minutes." I cleared my throat and Clarke lifted the paper towels off his face and began to sit up.

"No need to sit up, Mr. Clarke," Freeman told him.

"I'm okay." He was not, but he sat up anyway.

"This is Detective Freeman," I said. "From Coral Gables. He's handling this case."

Clarke looked like he was forming a question but said nothing.

Freeman nodded at me and turned to Clarke. "Tell me exactly what happened, starting with when, um," Freeman glanced down at his pad, "Mr. Steiner arrived in your office. Take your time, no detail is too small."

Clarke spoke for about three minutes, and I didn't hear anything that conflicted with what I'd heard and seen. According to Clarke, when Steiner discovered the transmitter, he ripped it off and then reached inside his coat for his gun. At the same time, Clarke pulled his own gun out of the desk drawer. "I don't know if he was going to shoot me, but I couldn't wait to find out."

"How did he find the bug?" Freeman asked.

"He reached over, really quick, and ran his hand up and down on my shirt."

"What do you think made him suspect that you were wearing a wire?"

I had been wondering the same thing.

Clarke shook his head. "I don't know. Maybe he realized he'd just admitted to killing my wife?"

Freeman nodded. "Is the Model 60 yours?"

"The what?"

"The revolver."

"Oh. Yeah. We have valuables here sometimes. Am I in trouble?"

"I don't think so, Mr. Clarke."

Freeman and I left the building together. "How are you going to call it?" I asked.

"Looks like self-defense. Your guy had every reason to believe that he was in mortal danger. His reaction was justified. I'll tell you, though, I wish he hadn't shot him right between the eyes."

"Yeah?"

"You find yourself involved in what amounts to an Old West quick draw, you're going to squeeze off as soon as the other guy is in front of the barrel. What are the chances of such a deadly shot?"

I swept my right hand up from under an imagined desk, gripping an imagined gun. "The gun is coming up out of a desk drawer and Steiner is leaning in. That makes his forehead the first thing in the line of fire."

Freeman tried the motion himself. "That could be. Anyway, two guns, no witnesses...I don't see what we could pull from the scene to prove a different story. Seems justifiable any way you look at it and that's how I'm going to write it up."

When we got to my car, there was a ticket on my windshield, the meter long expired. Freeman laughed and took it from my hand. "I'll take care of that. Give me your badge number."

I was drained by the time I got back to the station. I took a couple of Excedrin before briefing the lieutenant. He wasn't happy. I took what was left of my butt back to my desk and called Assistant State Attorney Cricket Nixon to tell her that Clarke had done an outstanding job of obtaining a taped confession, but we wouldn't be using it.

"He set that up."

"Excuse me?"

"He planned to kill Steiner from the start," she said. "He didn't think the justice system would handle it correctly, so he handled it himself."

"I was there," I told her. "Steiner discovered the wire after he had implicated himself. He pulled a gun and Clarke defended himself."

"I'm sure you're right," she said, but in a way that conveyed pity rather than agreement.

When I hung up, Wayne Thomas was sitting in the chair beside my desk. I showed the same kind of enthusiasm that I'd have shown an unfavorable termite inspection report. It didn't matter to Wayne; he had enough enthusiasm for both of us.

"You look like you just caught your best huntin' dog in the chicken coop."

"Not a good day," I agreed.

"What happened?"

Wayne ummed and ahhed and whistled a couple of times as I gave a quick run-down of the day's events.

"Bad," he agreed, "but there is an upside, dontcha think? It wraps up your Clarke case and without you spending one day in court."

"Yeah," I said, still bothered by Cricket Nixon's darker view.

"Of course," he continued, "it kind of makes my trip over here to see you wasted – except for the pleasure of your company."

I shook my pounding head. "Okay, Wayne, what have you turned up?"

"It can't be much now, but man oh man, it sure seemed interesting when I heard it." He stared away in mock deep thought.

"I'm not in the mood, Wayne."

"Gotta be a coincidence. I should just…"

"Wayne!" Half the squad room looked around.

Wayne looked shocked, then his face rearranged itself into an annoying grin. He is better at this than I am. "It's about my second burglar hypothesis."

"Imagine that."

"You remember that Walters' burglary I told you about?"

"The four-hundred-fifty-thousand-dollar necklace?"

"It was four-eighty, but yeah, that's the one."

"Okay…"

"The Walters have an alarm system which the service confirms was active. It never tripped and no signs of forced entry."

"Domestic."

"They employ one girl and she's been with 'em for 11 years."

"Family member."

Wayne did a little *comme-ci, comme-ça* motion with his left hand. "They weren't much interested in learning the who until their insurer denied the claim because there was no evidence of a break-in. That's when their story changed a bit."

"Are you getting close to the Mary Clarke part?"

"Indeed, I am. Their original story was that the necklace

disappeared between early Sunday morning and nine o'clock Monday morning – we're talking about the Monday morning before the Tuesday our Mary Clarke disappeared.

"The stolen necklace normally resides in a safety deposit box. On Friday, Mrs. Walters went to the bank to get it to wear that night to some gala event out at the Beach. Since she couldn't return it to the bank until Monday, she put the thing into a drawer in her jewelry chest. When she opened that drawer on Monday morning to retrieve it, the necklace was gone."

"So, it could have been stolen on Saturday."

"Exactly, and here is where it gets interesting. On Saturday, Mrs. Walters hosted about a dozen other ladies, mostly from the neighborhood, for an afternoon party. She didn't mention this before because she was afraid that it would appear that she thought one of them might have taken the necklace."

Now I understood the hand motion. "One of her friends stole her necklace?"

"Probably."

"And Mary Clarke was at the party?"

"You take all the fun out of it."

"You think Mary Clarke swiped a neighbor's necklace and someone killed her for it? I'm not seeing how that works."

"I just see a trail here, Stick. I don't know where it leads." Wayne paused and I knew there was more. "We got thumb and forefinger prints from the jewelry box that don't match the maid or anyone living in the house."

"Horkheimer has Mary Clarke's prints from processing her house. You can check, but I'll lay 20 bucks that you don't get a match."

Wayne shook his head and picked up the cassette lying on my desk. "No bet. Anyway, this and the killer in the morgue kinda closes this one, doesn't it?"

13

WEDNESDAY, AFTERNOON

I was shamelessly relieved that the department had already sent someone else to inform Herb Steiner's wife of her husband's death, but as I turned onto the driveway of the neat South Dade residence on Wednesday, I was still less than eager to speak with Wanda Steiner.

The Steiner home was in one of the newer neighborhoods, the kind with a wall around it and a guard house at the entrance – trying to keep out the bad element. Solidly upper middle class, the house featured a French roof line, but the color was South Florida. The open garage exposed a washer and dryer at the back, an overflowing laundry basket sitting on top of the dryer. In the middle of the garage floor was a red tricycle. Nearer to the wall was a pink bicycle with a wicker basket over the front wheel and streamers hanging from the handle grips.

Out of the car, I could hear the washer making a loud thumping noise and see a little trickle of water coming from under it in a contest against the heat to extend itself all the way to the driveway. A gray-and-white cat just inside the garage, frozen in the middle of grooming itself, eyed me warily as I went toward the front door. A little boy, about five, answered the bell.

"Is your mother home?"

Without a word, he streaked out of sight, leaving me standing at the open door.

"Yes?" The voice came from behind me and I turned to find a woman standing in the driveway. She must have come out into the garage to check on the wash and seen my car in the drive.

Wanda Steiner was about 35, maybe five feet three inches tall, and about 15 pounds overweight. Her brown hair was short and in tight curls all over her head. She had wide-set brown eyes, a pointed nose, and a very straight mouth. She was wearing a navy-blue dress, a little too tight in the hips, and black high heels. A curious outfit for doing laundry.

"Mrs. Steiner?"

"Yes."

"My name is Segal, Mrs. Steiner. Frank Segal. I'm a detective with Metro Homicide. I would like to talk with you for a few minutes if I could."

"About my husband?"

"Yes, ma'am."

"He was mixed up with drug dealers and now he's dead. So, I'm a widow and our kids don't have a father." She started to weep then and turned away from me to go back into the garage. I followed her and stood near the tricycle while she yanked the clothes from the washer and slammed them into the dryer. 'Damn him! Damn him! Damn him!" A shirt caught on the dryer door and dropped to the concrete, a man's shirt. She picked it up and fingered it as though it were expensive silk, then her face collapsed and she went into gut-wrenching sobs.

When she staggered, I stepped quickly forward and caught one arm. Clutching the damp shirt against her breast, she pivoted and buried her face in my chest. I stood as motionless as a wall while her sobs subsided into sniffs, feeling overwhelmingly sorry for her. I was glad she did not know I was the person who set up the meeting between her husband and the man who shot him.

"I'm sorry, Mrs. Steiner." My voice sounded thick. When I had seen her husband lying on the floor, I had felt only relief that it wasn't Roger Clarke, but Mrs. Steiner was reminding me yet again that our side doesn't have an exclusive on grief. I cleared my throat. "Can you tell me about your husband, tell me more about him? Will you talk to me?" I felt a nod of assent.

Inside, the house was spotless, except that a vacuum cleaner was sitting on the carpet in the living room, a mop and bucket sat in the middle of the kitchen, a dust cloth and Pledge were on the dining table, and the dishwasher door was open. Any activity to shut out the awful truth.

Sitting in the living room with the vacuum between us, Mrs. Steiner told me that they had married one month after graduating high school in New Brunswick, New Jersey, where Herb Steiner's father was a dry cleaner. When the father died, the business was sold, and with Herb's mother they had moved to South Florida. Herb opened a dry cleaner on Kendall Drive, just as apartments were being built there, and within a few years they owned a chain of stores. The business had not made them wealthy, but it provided a comfortable living for the growing family.

A friend had suggested to Herb a way of doing better, a lot better. Herb was already in deep when Wanda found out. She begged him to stop, but he refused.

"What was he doing?"

"Laundering the money."

"Right from the start?"

"Always. That was the only aspect of the business he wanted anything to do with. He used to tell everyone that the only business he had ever been in was the laundry business. Like it was a big joke, right."

"Who was he working for?"

She hesitated.

"Okay, we don't need to go there now. That's not why I'm here. I'm a homicide detective, Mrs. Steiner, but it's not your husband's death I'm investigating. It's a murder your husband claimed to have committed."

"Mary Clarke." Her matter-of-fact delivery shocked me.

"You know about Mary Clarke?"

"Only her name."

"You knew your husband killed her?"

"Of course not," she said. "Herbie never hurt anyone. Ever."

"He told Mary Clarke's husband that he killed her."

"So he says."

"No, ma'am. The conversation was being recorded."

"No."

I had the copy I had promised Harry Freeman in my jacket pocket. I held it up.

She looked at the cassette. "He really told that man he killed his wife?"

"Yes, ma'am."

She shook her head violently, trying to shake out the truth. "I don't believe he said that," she said, standing and leaving the room. She returned with a long, thin cassette player the color of an orange Life Savers.

"That's not a good idea, Mrs. Steiner."

She placed the machine on the coffee table, punched the load button, and glared down at me.

I slid the cassette into the open compartment and pushed it closed. I was not going to play the entire exchange, so I kept skipping through the tape with the fast-forward button, stopping only long enough to hear two or three words: "...ing side show frea...o much cash...have the balls to...another funeral...you that killed her." I stopped it there, knowing what was coming next and unsure that I was doing the right thing.

Wanda had been staring at the candy-colored recorder, listening very intently. She looked up at me now and read the hesitation in my face. "Go ahead," she said. "If it's on there, I have to hear it."

She already knew that it was there.

I punched the play button and the dead Herb Steiner snarled, "I just helped her over the bridge railing. And I'm only going to tell you one last time, you're about to kill your daughter the same way. Get me the fucking papers."

"Oh, God!"

The expletive came from across the room. Neither of us had heard her enter, had seen her standing near the doorway. She was not as tall as Cheri Clarke, but she was Cheri's age. Thin, with dark hair and a pixy face, she was wearing jeans and a man's white dress shirt with the tails out and the sleeves rolled up to her forearms.

"What the hell do you think..." Roger Clarke's voice startled me and I jabbed the stop button on the cassette player.

Wanda Steiner was already halfway across the room. "Helen."

The girl was backing toward the doorway and pushed at her

mother violently. "It's true," she cried. "It's all true. I hate him! I hate him! I'm glad he's dead!"

"Oh, Helen, you don't mean that. He…"

"I do mean it," she shouted. "I do! I wish I was dead, too!"

That brought me back to Cheri Clarke, and I wasn't liking my part in any of this. Then she did something that affected me far more than her words. She suddenly realized she was wearing his shirt. She grabbed the collar of it with both hands and, with the strength of her anger, jerked her hands apart. Buttons flew like popcorn from a hot skillet and the shirt fell open. She tore her arms out of it and threw it in a wad at her mother's feet. I could not fathom in a girl her age a hurt so deep, an anguish so complete, that it would compel this display in front of an unknown man. I was frightened for her.

Her mother reached out again, but Helen Steiner spun and ran from the room. Wanda Steiner stood for a time without moving, looking down at the cast-off shirt, the rent link between father and daughter. Then, very deliberately she picked up the shirt and followed her daughter out of the room.

She was gone for more than 20 minutes. During that time, the little boy who had answered the door reappeared and we got acquainted. He told me that his name was David and he was almost five. He told me that his daddy cleaned clothes.

When Wanda Steiner returned, her wide-set eyes were red but dry. There was a twitch in her jaw and her look had hardened. She took David off my knee and sent him to his room. He sensed her mood as well and took off without protest. She sat back down next to me.

"He was a great father," she started. "That's why he was

doing what he was doing, to give the kids more. He was already talking to me about buying her a sports car. She can't even get her license for three years. Now she's lost him. He's never going to know it, but the stupid son of a bitch has lost her as well."

I had no idea where this was going, so I just let her talk.

"We didn't need the money. I should have...." She was about to blame herself, but she stopped. "He wrote poetry for me. A lot of poetry." She went across the room to a small bookcase and came back with a photo album. Instead of photos, the clear pages held neatly penned poems. Most were love poems. Whether they were good or not I couldn't say, but they clearly painted a different picture of Herb Steiner than the one from the cassette in my jacket.

"Herbie didn't kill that woman. It doesn't matter what he says on that tape, he didn't kill her. If you believe him, whoever did kill that poor woman is going to go free."

"It isn't something he would be likely to tell..." I started, but she cut me off.

"I was there when he got the call."

"The call?"

"The one telling Herbie about Mary Clarke's murder, that she had been dropped into the bay with a concrete block tied to her feet, that an insinuation that the same thing could happen to the daughter would bring the husband around. The man was refusing to do something they wanted him to do."

"Do you know who was on the other end of the call?"

"Sure, Arturo Ribera."

I sat up straighter. "You heard this call?"

"Our side of it."

"You're saying that Arturo Ribera killed Mary Clarke? Or had her killed?"

"I don't know. Herbie tried to tell me Arturo had nothing to do with it, but we both knew what kind of person he is. So maybe."

"You know Arturo Ribera?"

"He's the friend that talked Herbie into this mess."

"Friend?" I challenged. "He's the reason your husband is dead."

"Yeah, and as a confessed murderer," she said. "Oh Herbie."

She sat quiet for a time, but then said, "I know more than they think I do. Can I give it to someone?"

"You need to think about that."

"No. I don't."

14

THURSDAY, MORNING

THE RUNNER BOATS FACTORY WAS IN ONE of the big industrial areas of Hialeah, close to the horse track. It was Arturo Ribera's company, begun when he was importing marijuana and needed a boat faster than anyone else's. Ribera had long since quit the pot trade for far more profitable cocaine. His shipments came in by air these days, not by boat and rarely into Dade County.

His Runner boats had a long-standing reputation for speed, particularly in rough waters, and that had made them popular with the jet set. Young studs were equally attracted to the Runner name and the boat's dark past, imagining themselves as modern day buccaneers.

Runner built only one model, a 39-foot deep-vee that many a drug enforcement agent and Coast Guard boat had seen only from the stern. U.S. Customs had been so pleased with two confiscated Runner boats that they had purchased a third one directly from Ribera. That earned some blistering editorials from Florida newspapers.

Boating publications were less outraged and had occasionally made Ribera out to be a folk hero. Romanticizing drug running to sell fast boats to dentists is no more reprehensible than much of contemporary advertising, but romanticizing Arturo Ribera was completely inexcusable. He put me in mind of a magazine article I had read recently detailing a scientific explanation for life – something about an intelligent slime crawling out of the ocean. Intelligent slime was a good description of Arturo Ribera and crawling out of the ocean is how we got him. Only it was not life that he brought with him.

Ribera had grown up on the streets in the meanest part of Medellín, Colombia, on his own from the age of six. That's reason enough to turn out bad, but not as bad as Ribera. He was known to have bragged that the first time he killed a man he was just seven. Since then, many people who crossed paths with Arturo Ribera turned up dead, or never turned up at all. Yet, after 15 years in the U.S., Ribera's criminal record was as clean as my grandmother's – maybe cleaner. Not even a traffic citation.

These days Arturo Ribera had little to do with Runner Boats, where I had just arrived, but he kept his office here. He now owned restaurants and other businesses in Miami and oversaw them from this second-floor space. A dark-skinned woman with square shoulders and big breasts sat behind a desk at the head of the stairs. She was occupied with a glossy Spanish celebrity magazine when I came up, but I was confident that the two cameras in the stairway had already announced my presence to the office. The wall beside her desk featured a framed poster-sized blowup of a cover of *Powerboat Magazine* with Arturo Ribera smiling at the camera from the helm of what must be a Runner boat.

When the woman looked up, I flashed my badge. She appraised it, looked up at me, then without a word gave up her chair to go toward the door to her left, wagging her ample rear end as she went. She tapped on the closed door, opened it, and was back immediately to wave me toward the office.

Ribera sat behind a marble desk as big as a snooker table. If he was looking for another victim, I could heartily recommend his decorator. The office was a study in tacky. A red nude stood on a black Grecian pedestal in one corner. In another, illumination inside a gold leaf curio cabinet with a wavy glass front gave off a greenish glow. It held a collection of stuffed hawks. A mounted hammerhead shark stretched the full width of the office at one end. Its boneless body was bent so that from anywhere in the office you were facing its gaping mouth with its multiple rows of razor teeth. Glass eyes in the grotesque stalks stared blindly at opposite walls. On the sofa beneath the shark slouched Jack Boggs.

Seeing Boggs didn't surprise me that much. He had claimed that he only knew Steiner casually, that they had been going somewhere else together when Steiner asked to stop by Roberts & Wilson for a minute. Of course, he had no idea what the stop was for. When he heard the shot, his reaction had been instinctive, not mercenary. Freeman did arrest him – felons aren't supposed to be whipping out a pistol regardless of the saintliness of the motivation – but he was probably out by the time I got back to the station.

Ribera pushed his chair back and stood up. He was about six two, a big-framed man, but he didn't carry one extra pound. His shiny black hair was combed straight back. Heavy black eyebrows shielded deep-set dark eyes. He was clean shaven, but his jaw was tinted with the dark shadow of a heavy beard barely under the control of his razor.

Beneath his dark head was a tailored light linen suit. His shirt was open at the collar and a single gold chain supported a medallion nestled into a thatch of black wool on his chest.

"Detective Segal, right?" A disarming smile spread across his face, incongruous with the hard eyes above it. I imagined other rows of teeth behind the bright white ones that showed.

"That's right."

"I'm Arturo Ribera. I believe you have already met Mr. Boggs." He extended a hand across the desk but I made no effort to reciprocate. The eyes never changed, but my snub took the smile off his face. "What is it you want?"

"I want to talk to you about your relationship with Herb Steiner."

"Relationship?"

"You did know Herb Steiner?"

"Of course. We have been friends for years."

"How long have you been in business together?"

Ribera lowered himself into his chair. "Sit down, Segal. I don't have a lot of time for this, so why don't you tell me why you're here and I'll see if I can help you. You could have called, you know, saved yourself a trip."

I was here because Arturo Ribera had been on the other end of the call to Steiner – if there had been a call. Steiner worked for Ribera; Boggs' appearance at Roberts & Wilson suggested it and Wanda Steiner had confirmed it. But Wanda couldn't allow her daughter to believe her father was a murderer, so what was said on that call? Did I really think Ribera was going to answer that?

I had a confession from a guy with a motive, so why had his widow's denial deflected me? And even if I decided Steiner didn't do it, I had little reason to suspect Ribera. Not that he wasn't capable, but why would he involve himself that deeply in

Steiner's part of the business? It made little sense.

So now what? I should have just cut my loss and walked out, but I didn't. I settled into one of the velvet chairs in front of Ribera's desk. "I do hope you can help me," I responded. "As his friend, maybe you can tell me why Herb Steiner confessed to murder."

"Herb runs a dry cleaner business. I have my suits cleaned there. He couldn't kill anyone."

"So why would he confess to killing Mary Clarke?"

"Is that the woman you fished out of the bay last week? Miami's finest thinks it was Herb who killed her?"

"You're not listening. I said he confessed to her murder. I didn't say he did it."

"He didn't confess either."

"No?" I nodded toward the sofa. "Didn't your goon there tell you how Steiner died? With a wire in his hand? But he discovered it too late." I reached into my jacket and pulled out the cassette. It made a plastic clatter as it bounced on the marble desk. Ribera never took his eyes off me, never looked at the cassette.

"Okay. So why tell me?"

"If you're right about your friend being innocent, that makes the way he died particularly tragic, leaving behind two kids and a grieving widow. You know Wanda? They had a great marriage, shared everything. Then this. The poor woman is inconsolable."

"Is there a point here?"

"She's also angry. Seems they were doing fine until a friend of theirs waved big money in front of Herb and lured him into the drug business. The same friend was supplying the money Herb was laundering. And when a problem came up, the same friend provided a solution – only it resulted in a transition from doting father and husband to confessed killer and corpse." My tongue made a clicking noise. "You really can't blame her for being mad. She insisted on coming down to the station and talking for hours. Gave us a long list of names. You're on it, other people you know."

"Forget about it, Segal. I couldn't care less what Wanda Steiner tells you. Whatever shit Herb was doing, now she wants to shift the guilt somewhere else. If it makes her feel better, good for her, but nothing she tells anyone is going to connect me with anything illegal. Everybody knows I did some smuggling back in the day. So did Joe Kennedy. So what? Today, I'm a businessman. Period."

I picked up the cassette and dropped it back into my coat pocket. "Save that bullshit for the press. We both know what you are. And the death of your stooge does not close this case. He wasn't the person I'm looking for."

I stood and his eyes followed me up unchanged, but his mouth slipped into a knowing smile. "I couldn't agree with you more. I hope you find the real killer."

At the door, I looked back and left him with a parting suggestion: "You should consider skipping Herb's funeral."

15

THURSDAY, MIDDAY

I WENT BACK TO THE STATION AND LOOKED OVER the information Wanda Steiner had given us. There were names that I hadn't heard before, but otherwise, what she "knew" and what she could testify to in front of a jury were two different things. If she was going to make any contribution at all to bringing Ribera down, it would have to be through one of the names we did not already have, which seemed doubtful.

Leaving Ribera's office, I had worried that my imprudent use of Wanda might have put her at risk, but when I saw how right Ribera was about her ability to connect him to anything, I saw no reason for him to cause her any more harm than he already had. It was a poorly drawn conclusion. My subconscious must have had a better grasp on reality because I decided to go by her house anyway to have another talk with her about being cautious – just in case.

There was a big Cadillac in the driveway when I got to her house, so I parked on the street. The garage was still open and as I approached, I could hear the insistent squawk of the alarm that announces the washing machine is out of balance. I half expected Wanda Steiner to come out of the door inside the garage to readjust the clothes. I was almost across the driveway when I heard a terrific crash inside the house. I stopped and dropped to a crouch in front of the Caddy. Heat poured from the car's grille; whoever was here had not been here long.

A second crash brought my gun into my hand. I ducked into the garage and went to the back door. The washer alarm was a problem. It would announce my entry if I opened the door with it buzzing. I checked the door to be sure it was unlocked, then pushed the dial to shut off the alarm. Flattening myself against the wall on the hinged side of the door, I waited to see if anyone would come to investigate.

I didn't have long to wait; another crash filtered through the closed door. Opening the door slowly, I entered the kitchen in a full crouch. From behind the end of the counter I didn't see anyone, but I heard gasping from farther inside.

"I don't think you had enough," a man growled.

"No! No! Please!" The second voice was Wanda Steiner's. Scuffling noises followed, then the sickening thud of a vicious punch mixed with a high-pitched cry of pain.

I quickly moved the length of the kitchen and looked around the corner, through the family room and into the living room. Jack Boggs stood in the center of the room with his back to me. He was holding Wanda Steiner up with a powerful grip on her upper arm, her lips both busted and blood flowing from her mouth. Her dress was ripped and blood-spattered. The side of her face was an angry red. She was looking away, shaking violently in anticipation of the next blow.

Four quick steps got me to the opening to the living room as Boggs drew back to hit her again. With both arms extended, I cocked the hammer of my Special. His head whipped around to see me standing with a two-handed grip, the barrel pointed right into his face.

"Police. Freeze," I said just above a whisper.

He read the rabid rage in my eyes and went still, releasing his grip on Wanda Steiner's arm. She collapsed like a discarded beach towel, then with a back-pedaling motion pushed herself away from Boggs and onto the hearth of the decorative fireplace. Without taking my eyes off Boggs, I asked Wanda if he was alone. She must have nodded at first and then realized that I wasn't looking in her direction because her "yes" was late coming.

"Hands on top of your head, Boggs. You won't be out so quick this time," I said.

"No? I wouldn't bet on it, Segal. I'm not carrying, and the wife of my close friend surely isn't going to press charges." He smirked at me, then took his eyes off mine for the first time since he had seen me in the room. "Are you Wan...?"

Even if I had seen her sooner, I couldn't have stopped her. I don't know whether it was because of what Boggs was saying, or delayed anger, or just because her hand bumped into the overturned tool stand when she was pushing herself away from him. Whatever the reason, when I first realized she was moving, she was already swinging the heavy fireplace poker.

Boggs' threatening look never reached Wanda. As he turned his head, the big, curved hook on the side of the flashing poker caught him in the center of the right eye. The heavy point of the tool crashed against Boggs' forehead with such force that the shock caused Wanda to lose her grip on the handle. Boggs and the poker hit the floor at about the same time, but the poker had gotten the better of the exchange.

Boggs curled into a fetal position, covering his face while he rocked, yelling "Fuck!" over and over between long screams. The blow she had delivered would have sent me on to the next life, but Boggs didn't lose consciousness. When he rolled up to his knees, his right hand cradling the gore of his destroyed eye, Wanda already had the poker in her hands again. I reached out and grabbed her wrist with my left hand.

"Enough!"

"The bastard! You bastard!" she screamed over his groans. "You think I won't press charges? You think I won't testify against you and Arturo? You think I'm afraid of you? You've already destroyed me. There's nothing else you can do."

Boggs was in serious pain, but his good eye found her and she spat in it.

"Goddamn it, she blinded me."

"Just one eye, Jack-o. Just one eye. But I'm considering giving this poker back to her and letting her finish the job."

His good eye reopened and found me this time. "What the fuck?"

"You bastard!" Wanda kicked out at him, but I had pulled her back just far enough that she missed.

"We get tired of filling out reports on you and then have you back on the street doing the same old shit. If I just turn my back long enough to let her take out the other eye, then I won't really give a shit if they cut you loose. You see what I mean, Jack-o?"

At that, Wanda quit squirming and stood quietly at my side, waiting to see if I was going to give her another swing for her quarter. Deep down, the idea appealed to me. Back when I was in uniform, I had been in trouble a couple of times for a brief bit of extra enthusiasm with my night stick. Both "victims" were the same: big, brutish husbands who had beaten their tiny wives into comas. It was a weakness of mine.

"You can't do that!"

"No? Against the rules, is it? So is beating the hell out of a woman half your size. So is tying a woman to a concrete block and dropping her into the bay. Maybe we just play by your rules for a while."

"I need a doctor." He was rocking, looking at the floor.

"So does Wanda, but she's willing to wait. Who killed Mary Clarke?"

"What? Jesus, I don't know." His good eye found me again. "You said Herb confessed."

"Wrong answer, Jack-o."

"I don't know. I never even heard of Mary Clarke before yesterday."

"You're lying."

"I'm not. I'm not." The adrenaline was wearing off and I was sure that the pain was starting to hammer through to his brain. He pulled one of his hands away and looked at the mess in it with his good eye. "Oh, shit. I need a fucking doctor, man."

"Not until I know about Mary Clarke."

"I'm telling you, I don't know nothing about that. What I gotta do to make you believe me?"

"Why are you here?"

"Arturo sent me. He told me to teach her a lesson about loyalty."

"Loyalty!" Wanda screamed at him. I squeezed her wrist hard. He was talking, and I wanted all I could get out of him.

"That tape player we used yesterday, can you record with it?"

"Yes."

"If I turn you loose, will you put the poker down and go get it? I promise you if he lies to us, I'll give you five minutes at him. This may be a chance to correct the record on Herb."

She turned the poker loose and it thudded to the floor. I released her wrist and she left the room, returning quickly with the little orange machine and a cassette. She loaded the machine and checked to make sure it was recording, then came back to my side and held it out in front of her.

I read Boggs the Miranda. He wisely declined an attorney. Then I asked him again the purpose of his visit and he repeated his answer.

"What business is Arturo Ribera in?"

"He owns a boat company."

"That's good. Take all the time you want to get your facts straight."

"You gotta call nine-one-one. You can't do this."

I had Wanda turn off the recorder and rewind it. "You want rules Jack-o, here they are. The attorneys can fight it out on whether or not this tape is admissible in court, but I'm not going to have you queer it by groaning and complaining and in general leading the listener to believe that you're not answering willingly. We can do it over and over until I'm happy with it, or we can do it right the first time. It doesn't matter at all to me; you decide." I nodded at Wanda, "Restart it."

We went through it again, Miranda and all, but this time when we got to the question of Arturo Ribera's business, Boggs said, "He's in the drug business."

"Meaning?"

"He imports drugs from other countries, mostly Colombia, and distributes them in this country."

"Illegal drugs?"

"Yeah, illegal drugs. Cocaine, crack, whatever is in demand."

"What do you do for Ribera?"

"Bodyguard, mostly. Sometimes I run errands, deliver messages."

"Like the one you just delivered to Mrs. Steiner?"

"Yeah, like that."

"What did Herb Steiner do?"

"He was an independent."

"What do you mean?"

Boggs flinched from a sudden rush of pain and released an involuntary groan. He cleared his throat on the end of it, masking it well. I gave him a cold look and asked the question again: "What do you mean, independent?"

"He worked for himself. He bought drug money at a discount, paying for it in clean money."

"For Ribera? He was laundering illegal drug money for Ribera?"

"Yeah."

"Did you kill Mary Clarke?"

"I never even heard of Mary Clarke until two days ago."

"If you work for Ribera, why were you with Steiner the day he was killed?"

"He had asked Arturo if he could borrow some muscle for his meeting. Arturo sent me, but he told me not to get involved."

"Did Herb Steiner kill Mary Clarke?"

"I don't know." He flinched again, but he was silent this time.

"What do you think?"

"No."

"Why not?"

"Not the type. He tried to act tough, but he was scared all the time. No way he could snuff some woman. No way."

"Maybe he had it done?"

"Same thing. No way."

"How about Ribera?"

"You mean could he, or did he?"

"Both," I said.

"He could but he didn't."

"You sound positive."

"I am."

"You know everything he does?"

"No. But I know why he does things. Never without a reason. He had no reason to kill that woman."

"To help out Steiner?"

"Arturo wouldn't do it."

"He loaned you out," I pointed out.

"Not the same thing. There's no risk in me riding along with Steiner. There's big risk in disposing of some corporate wig's wife. Arturo is cautious, real cautious. He wouldn't be involved in the Clarke woman's death."

I asked him a few more questions, but my humanity finally came dragging back into the front of my mind and I shut off the recorder and called for a couple of ambulances.

Boggs went eagerly, and a patrolman responding to the call rode along with him. Wanda flatly refused to go to the hospital.

The paramedics checked her over and told her she needed to have her cheek X-rayed. She promised that she would go to her own doctor, so they did what they could to make her more comfortable and left without her.

It was almost two hours before we were the only two left in the house. For the last 30 minutes we had had the company of a young patrolman waiting on the wrecker to show up to impound Boggs' Caddy. While he was there, Wanda Steiner was again in her cleaning mode, reconstructing the living room and showing remarkable stamina for a woman who had just been used as a punching bag. When the young officer left, Wanda sat down across from me and watched silently as I finished my report. When I looked up, she was crying.

"Are you okay?" I asked.

"I hurt."

"You should've let them take you to the hospital."

"I don't mean that way. I mean inside. I keep hoping I'll wake up, that this is all a bad dream. But it isn't, is it?"

I looked at the floor without answering. The right side of her face was terribly swollen and she had tired of holding ice to it. It had to hurt too, but everything is relative.

After a minute she said, "That's why I hit him. Not because of what he did to me. Because of what they did to Herbie. Will that tape really help against Arturo?"

"Probably not," I answered. "It helps me, but I don't think it will ever see the inside of a court room."

"You think he was telling the truth?"

"I don't know. Maybe."

"But tape recordings aren't good evidence?"

"It depends on the tape and the circumstances under which it was obtained. They will claim duress and win."

"What about a taped telephone conversation?"

It was not a hypothetical question, and a little trickle of electricity ran up my spine. "Why?"

"I got to thinking about it last night. Arturo called and Herbie had the answering machine on. When he heard it was Arturo, he picked up, but left the machine in the record mode, something he often did so he could go back and verify numbers and times."

"You have a recording of that conversation between Arturo and Herb?"

"We just use the same cassette over and over. I didn't think it would still be on there, but I played it last night and there it was."

"My, my," I said, a smile spreading across my face.

"I guess you want to hear it?"

"Please."

When she came back, she was loading a mini cassette into a hand-held Dictaphone. She re-wound the tape, then hit the play button. After a couple of other messages played, after about the third electronic beep, the unmistakable voice of Ribera said, "This is Arturo. I have…"

There was a clicking sound, then Herb Steiner said, "Hey Arturo. What's happening?"

"Are you still having a problem with that Clarke character over at Roberts & Wilson?"

"Yeah. I don't think he's going to come around. He must be a deacon or something."

"Maybe not."

"What?"

"Doesn't matter. I have a solution for you."

"I'm open to suggestions."

"Someone dumped the guy's wife off the Card Sound Bridge last week. He has a teenage daughter. Call him up and tell him the same thing could happen to the girl. He'll do anything you want."

"You killed his wife?"

"Watch your mouth! I said *someone* killed her. It doesn't matter who it was."

"Wait a minute, Arturo. I don't want to get involved in anything like this."

"Did you kill her?"

"You know I didn't."

"Then all you have to do is say, 'The same thing could happen to your daughter.' It doesn't involve you at all. Just friendly advice. You'll be helping him out."

"I don't know."

"Jesus." Ribera pronounced it like it started with an H. "I don't know why I have anything to do with you. If you can't handle…"

"Okay, Arturo. I'll take care of it."

"You'll see. After you lean on this guy and he folds, you're going to be feeling so good that Wanda will be calling me to thank me." The laughter was the locker room variety. "Let me know how it goes."

"Sure."

Receivers clicked and the next message started before Wanda turned it off.

16

THURSDAY, AFTERNOON

I DROVE WANDA STEINER TO HER DOCTOR. The X-rays showed no fractures, but she wasn't going to win any beauty contests for a while. I wondered what her daughter was going to think when she saw her mother.

When the doctor was through with her, Wanda rode back to the station with me to swear out a complaint against Boggs. While she was there, I thought it would be a good idea for her to talk to the State Attorney's office. I called to see if Cricket Nixon was still in the office and to confirm that it was still her case. She agreed to meet Wanda and said she would be at the station in about half an hour.

We met in the same third-floor conference room where we had prepared Roger Clarke, and I was sure the irony of that wasn't lost on ASA Nixon. After the introductions, I gave her a brief synopsis of what transpired at the Steiner home, leaving out my threats to Boggs and failing to mention how long I waited to call an ambulance. Both spontaneously and at inquiries from Nixon, Wanda affirmed my recount. She appeared as much partner as complainant.

Nixon noticed our odd rapport and gave me a look. She knew that I had been the one responsible for setting up the ill-fated meeting between Wanda's husband and the man who had killed him, making Wanda and me unlikely allies. She must have wondered if Wanda knew the part I had played. I hoped she wouldn't mention it.

I let her look through my copy of Wanda's statement to Vice on the previous day, promising to get her a copy as soon as we had the transcription. Then I played the Boggs tape for her. She made a few notes but no comments. When it finished, I played the telephone conversation. She asked me to play it a second time. When she was satisfied, she turned to Wanda and asked her if she was in the room when the conversation was taking place.

Wanda confirmed that she was and had heard the entire exchange.

"Good."

"I'll testify against all of them," Wanda said.

"Thank you. If we get to that point, we will be counting on you to do just that."

"What does that mean, 'if we get to that point'?"

"Arturo Ribera is a difficult person to get into court."

"But what about everything I know?" Wanda looked toward me for support.

Nixon also looked at me, but hers was a look of disapproval. She turned back to Wanda. "Did you ever see Arturo Ribera commit a crime? Money or drugs changing hands? Anything like that?"

"He told Herbie a lot of things."

"Stories, Mrs. Steiner. That's not evidence."

"But Arturo *is* in the drug business."

"I know that. But to convince a jury we need evidence, eye

witnesses. Your information may help us, but for now you have done all you can."

Wanda went quiet. Nixon reached across the table and placed her hand on top of Wanda's and said, "I'm sorry. We will put Jack Boggs in jail. All I can promise you about Ribera is that we'll do the best we can."

I asked Nixon to wait a few minutes and I took Wanda downstairs and found her a ride back home. Then I poured up a couple of cups of coffee and went back up to the conference room. Nixon was looking over other parts of the file when I got back. She thanked me for the coffee.

"Listen, I don't want you to get blindsided. Boggs is going to claim that I delayed getting him medical attention, that I interrogated him first."

"I know."

"He's already made a statement?"

"How old do you think I am, Segal?"

I might have guessed 28, but it's not the kind of question that you answer, so I didn't.

"Good," she said. "And you're not going to know, but I've been doing this for more than 15 years, so I was pretty sure he hadn't had a sudden rush of guilt and mistook you for the father confessor."

"Fifteen years?" I was incredulous.

"Not here, but yes."

"I wouldn't have even been close."

In a burst of quick, honest laughter, she said, "We're going to get along good."

"So, what've we got? Can you do anything with any of it?"

"I don't know," she answered. "Where does this leave you on Mary Clarke?"

"The only person who thinks Steiner killed Mrs. Clarke is Mr. Clarke."

"You don't believe Steiner's confession?"

"No."

"Ribera had her killed?"

"I doubt it. Boggs is right about it being a pointless risk. Clarke was Steiner's problem, not Ribera's."

"Maybe as a favor?"

"You ever met Ribera?"

"No."

"He doesn't do favors, certainly not for someone like Steiner."

"Well, we might be able to link him to Steiner's laundering with this telephone conversation. I'll let you know how it goes." She started gathering up papers and putting them in her briefcase.

I thanked her for coming and walked with her to the elevator. The one going down arrived first and she stepped into an empty car. As the door closed, she stuck out her hand and stopped it. "Segal? Eventually you're going to find out that Clarke set up Steiner."

The door re-closed before I could respond.

*   *   *

I sat straight up in bed, instantly wide awake. Herb Steiner's poetry. *Damn.* The clock on the desk said 4:30 a.m. I tried to go back to sleep, but Cheri Clarke kept jumping into the pool again, over and over. Finally, about 5:30, I got up, took a long shower, and drove to Benny's.

Benny's used to be a Royal Castle hamburger place. It's still white with a pair of orange stripes around it, and the tile at the entry still says Royal Castle, but Benny Agüera has been running a little diner there for 10 years. I ordered a steak, hash browns, and a large glass of fresh orange juice. Benny slid the hot plate onto the counter and sat a new bottle of ketchup next to it. He's the only person to make breakfast for me regularly since Pam left.

We talked about UM baseball, the latest tax hike coming out of Tallahassee, a tropical depression near Puerto Rico. He kept refilling my juice glass and, as always, when I was ready to leave, he refused to give me a bill. As always, I left money on the counter.

It was still too early for traffic, the only benefit of being up this early. I was at my desk before seven and sat looking at the cassette for several minutes, not sure I wanted to know. I opened my desk drawer a half-dozen times. His desk was different.

Finally, I loaded the cassette into the player and put the earphone in my right ear. I played it through until I reached the part I was listening for. I could not tell so I backed the tape up and played the last part again, this time with my index finger jammed into my left ear to cut out the noise of the squad room. Maybe.

The lieutenant wasn't in yet, so I took the player into his office, closed the door, and played the last part over and over in the quiet. Eventually my brain got all the sounds sorted out and I heard it, the sound I didn't want to hear.

At 7:30, I called Wanda Steiner at home. She sounded awful and told me that her lips had cracked and bled in the night, making it difficult for her to talk. I promised to be brief. "The poems you showed me, Herb's poems, did he actually write those?"

"Of course." She seemed affronted.

"I don't mean were they original," I clarified. "Was it Herb who wrote them on the paper? Is that his handwriting?"

"Oh. Yes."

"Herb was left-handed?"

"Yes."

Strike two. "Okay, Wanda. Thanks."

"Wait! Why are you asking?"

"It's nothing," I lied. "I'm just trying to get some reports finished. Thanks. And keep your doors locked."

"Yeah, I am."

My next call was to Coral Gables. The desk sergeant on duty told me Harry Freeman was not due in until 9:00, so I left a message. At 8:20, Freeman returned my call.

"You're in a little early, aren't you?" I chided.

"And when exactly does your shift start?"

"Touché. It started early today. Can you work me in for a few minutes?"

"About the Steiner case? Sure. Come on out."

My second encounter with traffic this morning was not as pleasant, but I eventually arrived at the Coral Gables Police Department. Freeman met me at the front desk and led me down a long hallway smelling of fresh paint and into a small office with a round table and a half-dozen chairs.

"Okay. What's up?" he asked.

"Steiner was left-handed."

"Shit!" The implications were not lost on him.

"Do you remember where his holster was?"

"Sure. It was on the right."

"What do you make of that?" I asked.

"It was a very nice holster," Freeman recalled. "Maybe that was more important than function. A left-hand model wasn't available? Maybe he just preferred it on the right."

"But if you didn't know, like Clarke didn't know, you would conclude that he was right-handed. That's where you would plant the gun."

"Plant the gun? Wait a minute, Segal. You're jumping to conclusions here, aren't you?"

"You're the one who said you wished Clarke hadn't shot him directly between the eyes. Remember?"

"Sure, and I remember this, too." He made the sweeping motion with his right hand that I had made after the shooting to brush aside his concern about the accuracy of Clarke's shot.

"There's something else," I said. I had already put the recorder on the table and I pushed it towards him. "When I listen to the tape, I hear Clarke open the drawer before the wire is discovered."

He listened. He replayed it several times. Finally, he stopped, holding the earphone in his hand, staring at it as though it were the key to a complex puzzle. "I don't know. Maybe. Maybe he's just moving his chair."

"I think that after Steiner told Clarke that he killed his wife, which, by the way, he didn't do, then Clarke..."

"Wait a minute! Wait a minute! Steiner didn't kill Mary Clarke?"

"No."

"What the hell?"

I told him about the call to Steiner from Ribera.

"Ribera killed her?"

"Probably not."

Freeman stared at me while he took in this new information. "Then who?"

I shook my head. "I don't know."

"Does Clarke know this?"

"No. Unless he killed her himself, he thinks Steiner did it. He undoubtedly feels justified in what he did."

"And you were about to say what that was."

"Steiner leaned forward and told Clarke that he had personally tossed Mary off the bridge. When he sat back, Clarke opened a drawer and pulled out his loaded .357. He motioned to Steiner to be silent, and Steiner was so far out of his element that he had no idea what was going on.

"Then Clarke ripped open his own shirt, protesting at the same time for the benefit of the mike. Steiner suddenly realized that he had been set up and started to say something, but Clarke ripped the wire loose. The way it plays in my head, Clarke says something to Steiner to let him know that he was about to die. Then he squeezes the trigger."

"That's a hell of an accusation."

"Nixon knew it immediately, and I should have."

"Who?"

"The ASA on the case. It doesn't matter. After the shot, it took me a while to get Boggs under control. I think Clarke went around the desk, put the torn wire in Steiner's left hand, pulled the automatic out of Steiner's holster and wrapped his right hand around it, then let it fall to the floor. By the time I got into the office, he was back in the chair looking like he was in shock."

We sat in silence for a few minutes while Freeman chewed vigorously on the dull end of a cheap ballpoint pen. He finally removed it from his mouth and shook his head. "I don't know, Segal. Just for the sake of argument, let's say that the sound on the tape is not the drawer. Even if it is, maybe he opened it because he was getting nervous about Steiner, but let's say it isn't the drawer."

"Okay," I agreed.

"Steiner leans into Clarke's face and confesses..." Freeman paused to shake his head, "to a murder he didn't commit. For some reason, it suddenly occurs to him that Clarke might be wired. He's left-handed, so with his left hand he pats Clarke's chest, feels something, rips open the shirt, and tears off the wire."

Freeman held a closed left hand out in front of himself. "The wire is now in his left hand. He has no reason to think Clarke is dangerous – if he was worried about Clarke, he'd have had Boggs in the office with them. So, with his free hand, the right one, he reaches for his gun. Clarke sees the gun, panics, pulls his own and fires." His right hand made my sweeping motion one more time. "Lucky shot."

"It could've gone that way," I admitted.

"But you don't like it?"

"Why does Steiner pull a gun at all? It's already too late to take back what he's said. Shooting Clarke, or even threatening him, is just going to make it worse."

"He doesn't know you're sitting in the next office monitoring the conversation. He thinks Clarke is recording on his own and he wants the tape."

Steiner was clearly an amateur, a virgin, one of Ribera's sacrificial lambs. Freeman could be right.

"You're going to let your report stand like it is?" I asked.

"I'll mention that Steiner was left-handed."

"Clarke could be getting away with murder."

"He wouldn't be the first one. Look, Segal, we could just as easily have had Clarke in a box and Steiner out on the street. Whatever happened in that office, Clarke did us a favor."

"You'll forgive Steiner's wife and kids for not agreeing with that assessment." I regretted it as soon as I said it. "Hey, listen, I'm sorry. It's your call. And you're damn sure right about the way it could have turned out."

Freeman just smiled. "This case has really got you torqued. Clarke has kids, too, doesn't he?"

"Yeah, two." I didn't tell him that one of those kids was the most persuasive argument for me to accept his version of how Steiner died.

17

FRIDAY, MIDDAY

I DROVE BACK EAST TO THE STATION trying to shake off a sense of
complicity. It was not my case, and I had given my suspicions to
Freeman. It was all I could do.

Wayne Thomas was watching for me when I came in,
slouched in the chair next to my desk. Before I even had a chance
to look at my telephone messages, he launched right into his
reason for the visit. "I swear, I think after this, they're going to
move me to Homicide."

"Uh-huh." One of the messages was from Cricket Nixon. I
picked up the receiver and dialed the number on the yellow sheet.

"Cricket?" Wayne had his neck twisted in an unnatural way
to read the message and I gave him a drop-dead look. "Well, I
can see that this is important. I'll just get us a couple of cups of
coffee to talk over police business when you get through there."

He got up to leave and I wadded up the message and hit him
on the side of the head with it. I don't know why I encourage him.

By the time Wayne returned with the coffee, I had talked
with someone else in the State Attorney's office and learned that
ASA Nixon would be in court until late this afternoon. I left a
message.

This time Wayne sat like a church mouse. He had already

given me all the clues I needed. It was clearly, in his mind, my turn. I fussed with the sugar, stirred until little bits of Styrofoam floated to the surface, fished them out, sipped the coffee, and sorted through other messages on my desk. The only sound that came from the side of my desk was occasional sipping. Finally, I pushed my chair back and swiveled around to face him.

"Okay, Wayne, why are they going to move you to Homicide?"

The church mouse grinned. "Dang, Wayne, he did hear you. They're going to move me to Homicide, Stick, because that's where those of us with crime-solving talents are supposed to be."

It was my turn to be silent.

"Don't you want to know which murder Detective Thomas has solved?"

"Jimmy Hoffa?"

"Hey, I do have a theory on that one. There was this picture in the *Herald* weeks ago, of a trial in Argentina – for some politician or general or something – and there was this one judge on the panel that looked just like Hoffa. I figure Hoffa took a lead from the Nazis, cleaned out the pension fund, flew to South America, and established a new identity. Now he's a high-court justice, rules on all extraditions. Anyway, now that I know he's still alive, it ain't a murder anymore, so I've lost interest."

"So have I."

"You'll get real interested again when you hear what I've found out."

"And exactly when is that?"

"You mean what?"

"That, too."

"You remember the burglary case I'm working on?"

"The half-million-dollar necklace?"

"It's four-eighty," Wayne corrected. "And you remember telling me to check with Horkheimer for Mary Clarke's prints?"

"I remember all of it, Wayne, including the value of the necklace. So, you went to see Horkheimer and...?"

He just looked at me with his mouth slightly open, sad-eyed, as though I was missing the whole point. "I went to see Horkheimer and came back with a full set of prints that match the partial on Stacy Walter's jewel case."

"Mary Clarke stole the necklace?" He did have my attention.

"Hold your horses, Stick. You're out of the gate too quick, jumping to an unwarranted conclusion." Wayne was the second person to tell me that today. "I didn't say anything about the prints belonging to Mary Clarke."

"Devereaux?" It was almost a squeak. Maybe Henry and Stacy Walters had their pool serviced by Pristine Pools.

Wayne sat upright in the side chair. "Devereaux? Let me see your phone messages."

"What?"

Instead of responding, he reached across my desk and picked up the small pile of messages. He flipped through them, pulled one out, and handed it to me. It was from an Officer Constanza.

"You didn't call this one?"

"I didn't call any of them."

He pointed at the wad of paper on the floor. "You called Cricket."

"How the hell do you know about my calls?"

"You know Constanza?"

"I don't think so."

"You want to call him, or do you just want me to tell you why he called?"

"How do you know why he called?"

"Because I told him to call you."

"You're making me crazy, Wayne."

Both hands came up in front of him. "Take it easy. Devereaux is right now a patient at Baptist Hospital. Dean Constanza is the investigating officer. When I heard about it, I thought you would want the details, so I asked him to give you a call."

"Baptist Hospital? Why?"

"With how fond you are of Devereaux, you are absolutely going to love this." Wayne started laughing.

I picked up the receiver. "I'll call Constanza..."

"No. Wait, wait," Wayne gasped. "I'll tell you."

I put the receiver down.

"This happened Tuesday, or was it Wednesday? Doesn't matter. Your pal, Devereaux, was at one of his longer appointments when hubby returned home, unexpectedly – and quietly. The husband had seen the pool service truck and when he didn't see anyone out at the pool, he walked down the hall. And from outside his own bedroom door, he heard what sounded like some very heavy-duty pump servicing."

"Move it along."

"So, it plays out typical from here. The husband goes back out to his car, retrieves a pistol from the glove box, and bursts into the bedroom. The wife screams and Devereaux starts scrambling around the room, trying to find an exit. The husband ignores the wife and corners Devereaux. He centers the pistol on Devereaux's chest, moves it a little right, and pulls the trigger. His aim is perfect." Wayne let out another hearty laugh.

"Jesus, Wayne. There's nothing funny about this."

"Wait. You haven't heard the punch line yet. Our husband volunteers as a referee for high-school sports. The pistol is a starting gun. Devereaux is in the hospital because when the gun went off, he jumped back right through the sliding glass door and shattered his own elbow. He'll be fine, but he's gonna have a big bare spot on the left side of his chest for a long time to remind him how close he came."

I did smile, but I felt strangely sorry for Greg Devereaux. "So, what does he have to say about Mrs. Walters' necklace?"

Wayne regained his composure and said, "What? Oh, no, Devereaux didn't have anything to do with the Walters' burglary."

"I thought you said…"

"No. You brought up Devereaux. The prints on Mrs. Walters' jewel case weren't Devereaux's, they belong to someone else."

"Who?"

"That's exactly what I wanted to know."

I shook my head and bit my tongue.

"All I really knew," he continued, ignoring my irritation, "was that the same person had been in both houses. Not exactly hot news. I mean, these ladies undoubtedly had mutual friends. And their friends aren't the kind of people whose prints are on file – or so I thought."

"Keep going, Wayne."

"Well, our jewel thief had already turned to crime at age 17, arrested for shoplifting from the cosmetics counter in a Memphis Woolworth. Her name was Marsha Anne Tucker."

Wayne waited for me to put it together. It took longer than

it should have, but I got there eventually. "Marsha Goodwin?"

"You got it."

"You think Marsha Goodwin stole the necklace?" I was trying to remember the inside of her house, the tasteful and expensive decor.

"I did a little checking. She's been divorced for about five years. Last year, her ex-husband went bankrupt and cut off all support payments. She has completely depleted her savings and is two months behind on her mortgage. The woman is in a deep financial hole. On the strength of that distress and her prints on the jewel case, we went out to her house yesterday afternoon with a search warrant."

"And?"

"And buried in a canister of rice in her kitchen, we found Stacy Walters' necklace."

"No shit!"

"Yeah. And it gets weirder."

I was still trying to picture the hoity-toity Ms. Goodwin as a jewel thief when I realized Wayne was awaiting a prod. "Go on."

"We brought her in, but she refused to talk to us. She made a call. And who shows up an hour later to bail her ass out? Mrs. Stacy Walters."

"Yeah," I nodded. "She'll want to withdraw her complaint, say she forgot she loaned it to Marsha. Pretend nothing ever happened."

"Yup. She called this morning."

I turned back to my desk.

"That's it? This doesn't interest you?" Wayne protested.

"Sure, it interests me. But it doesn't have anything to do with

Mary Clarke."

"Steiner's confession checked out?"

I snorted. "Despite his personal claims to the contrary, Herb Steiner had no part in the death of Mary Clarke." I was starting to talk like Wayne.

"Aha!"

"No! Not aha! Because Steiner didn't do it is not a reason to suspect Marsha Goodwin."

"You got weasel tracks in the henhouse and one of the chickens turns up missing, you got to figure that maybe the weasel did it."

"Marsha's prints are all over the house because she's taking care of Mary Clarke's kids. She's Mary Clarke's next-door neighbor. She probably has a key to the Clarkes' house. It is curious that she stole a necklace from a mutual friend three days before Mary's disappearance, but that's all, just curious. And the jump from theft to murder is a long one."

"Did she ever take care of the kids before?"

"Why?"

"Maybe it's a guilt reaction."

"Come on, Wayne. There's no way that Marsha Goodwin walked into Mary Clarke's house, knocked her in the head, dragged her out to the car, hauled her down to Card Sound and pitched her off the bridge, and you know it."

"Yeah, I guess. She's not exactly what I had in mind when I started looking for the second burglar. But living right next door to the Clarkes…." He trailed off, turning it loose with some difficulty. Satisfied, he leaned my way. "So, then, who did kill her?"

"I wish the hell I knew. Maybe Arturo Ribera, but I don't

really think so. Devereaux remains a remote possibility. Roger Clarke may have had the strongest motive, and the more I know about him, the more convinced I am that he is capable. If not Clarke, then maybe it was a player I don't even know about."

"A third burglar?" Wayne offered.

We both laughed.

*   *   *

I glanced at my watch when my telephone rang. It was just after 4:30. "Segal."

"Frank, it's Cricket."

The familiarity did not go unnoticed. I accepted the invitation to be friends. "Hey, Cricket. Tough day in court?"

"Five hundred."

"Five hundred?"

"I won one and I lost one."

"Got it. Is something happening on Ribera?"

"Yes and no. We met on the tapes this morning."

"We?"

"The state attorney and other staff. The consensus is that we won't be able to get the Boggs tape admitted."

"I'm not surprised."

"Uh-huh. However, it might still be useful, as a lever before we go to trial. The answering machine recording of Steiner and Ribera should be admissible, but Ribera doesn't really say enough to seriously incriminate himself. Maybe later, as a part of a more complete package."

"Kind of how I thought it would play. Sorry."

"No, it's good." The line went quiet for a couple of seconds, then she said, "Reid Katz called me this morning, asking about you."

"Reid Katz? About me?" Reid Katz was Miami's highest-profile defense attorney. Every major city in America must have a Reid Katz. It was hard to turn on the local news for five days in a row and not see Reid defending some off-the-wall religious cult, a daycare operator charged with child abuse, a terrorist, a fire bomber, or a mass murderer. They're all entitled to a legal defense, but Reid made a sideshow of it.

"Why?"

"He's representing Boggs. He's threatening a police brutality charge."

"Reid Katz is representing Boggs?" It was a role I could not place Katz in.

"He's Ribera's attorney."

"Ah."

"Could he make his case?" she asked.

"For brutality? I don't see how. I never laid a hand on Boggs. Fact is I kept Wanda Steiner from killing him. Despite her objections, I had a whole sequence of pictures taken of Wanda's face when she was at her doctor's office. I could have kicked his teeth down his throat, and with one look at those pictures the board would find it justifiable force. But I didn't. The only one who hit him was Wanda, and I would have stopped her if I could've."

"Good. That's what I told him. I also told him that we had a taped telephone conversation between Ribera and Steiner in which Ribera tells Steiner about the murder of Mary Clarke. I said that he might want to forget about throwing up a smoke screen around Boggs and work on his murder defense for the guy paying the bill."

I couldn't help but smile. I could imagine Reid's inflated face flushed with anger at the cheekiness of this Assistant State Attorney. "How did that play?" I asked.

"Better than I hoped. That's why I'm late calling you. I had a message from Katz when I got into my office, and I just got off the phone with him. Ribera is involved in some kind of legitimate business acquisition and the other principals are nervous about his reputation."

"They should be."

"The last thing Ribera wants right now is his name linked to a murder. Ribera told Katz that he recalled the conversation with Steiner, that it took place on Monday evening, right after the local news. That was the day the news reported that the body found the previous Friday was Mary Clarke. The only thing he knows about Mary Clarke's death is what he's seen on the news."

"I think I knew this, but what kind of a sociopath sees that story as an opportunity?"

"Every time someone blows up an airport or a bus, a half dozen groups claim credit for it."

"Yeah, I know. I never could figure Ribera for this murder. I'll see if Wanda can confirm when the call came in. What did Reid want for his goodwill gesture?"

"Well, first there's more goodwill. They're not contesting Boggs' arrest. He will plead guilty to assault and battery."

"Boggs is okay with that?"

"I don't think he has a say. You live by the sword. My part was just to not link Ribera to the Clarke murder in any statements to the press."

"That wasn't likely to happen anyway, but even appearing to be playing a role in sanitizing Ribera's reputation kind of leaves me with a bad taste."

"Uh-huh. Well, I got what I could..."

"No, I don't mean that," I interrupted. "You've done terrific. It puts an end to the bullshit brutality claim, and it saves me wasting any more time on Ribera. I just hate dealing with the devil."

"Who said *you* were?"

"What?"

"I made it very clear to Katz that I was speaking only for the State Attorney's office."

"He knows the department will comply."

"But no one has control over Wanda Steiner."

I held the receiver away from my ear for a moment and stared at it, my eyes and mouth crinkling into a smile. I brought the mouthpiece close again and said, "Well, now that could be a problem. I mean, I can certainly have a conversation with Ms. Steiner about what exactly she should not say to the press, but she might not listen to me."

A bit of a chuckle came across the line. "All anyone can ask, Detective Segal, is that you do your very best."

"I'm damn glad you're on our side," I said, hoping my sincerity would survive the electronic transmission.

She didn't respond, so I went on. "Cricket, there's something else."

"Yes?"

"I think you were right about Roger Clarke." I told her about Steiner being left-handed, about the drawer opening first, about my conversation with Freeman.

"Freeman could be right," she said.

"Yeah, maybe."

"Forget it, Frank. If he did it, he got away with it. If he didn't, he's damn lucky to still be alive. Either way, you can't do anything about it."

It was good advice, but she hadn't breathed life into Cheri Clarke or watched Helen Steiner's world collapse. Forgetting about it was never going to happen.

18

SATURDAY, MORNING

IT WASN'T THAT LONG AGO THAT A BARKING DOG in the neighborhood was what woke you up too early on a Saturday morning. Now it's someone's car alarm. The thing that hasn't changed is that the owner sleeps right through all the racket.

The barking alarm was on the next street, but my bedroom is in the back and the windows were open. The noise pierced my always fragile bubble of sleep. I tried to shut it out and go back to sleep, but to no avail. So, I just laid there for a while with the sheet tossed off, letting the ceiling fan pour cool morning air over my body, my wrists hanging off opposite sides of the big, empty bed.

"Well, what are we going to do today?" In the last couple of years, I had taken up talking to myself on my days off. This morning, the tragedy of that swept over me like the air from the fan, the tears that welled in my eyes catching me off guard.

I sat up, disgusted. "What the fuck is your problem, Segal?" A cold shower drowned my feelings, and I went to the kitchen wearing my towel and started a pot of coffee. Halfway back through the living room, I stopped and looked around. It was brown. Everything in the room was brown. Beige walls, tan carpet, brown furniture.

The living room Pam and I had shared had been like a fruit

salad – colors like peach, apricot, and strawberry. Lots of frills, pleats, and lace. Every room in the house had been like that, soft, feminine, splashed with color. Every room but one. There the white walls awaited the decision of pink or blue. A lonely panda sat patiently in one corner of the empty room.

I went back to my bedroom and pulled the telephone book from the bottom desk drawer. There were a dozen Kelseys listed, but only one Cristine Kelsey. I already had six digits dialed before I glanced at the clock and realized that it was just barely 7:30. I hung up, wrote the number on a piece of paper, and put the book back in the drawer.

Back in the kitchen, the car alarm and the percolator had a little jam session going and I joined in, tapping my spoon against the Formica counter while I waited for the coffee to finish. Breakfast was served up by the toaster.

At 8:00 I started the lawn mower. I began where Carmen had interrupted my mowing on the previous Saturday, but it didn't matter because the whole lawn had to be done. By 8:30 I was back in the house, picking up, straightening up, cleaning. I thought about Wanda Steiner, at that very moment wearing out her carpet with the vacuum cleaner.

Five minutes before nine I decided it was late enough and dialed the number on the piece of paper. A female voice answered.

"Cristine?"

"No. This is Patty."

"Is Cristine there?"

"Sure. Hold on."

The receiver clattered against the top of something and I could hear her shouting for Cristine. There was the click of a second receiver being lifted off the hook and a husky voice said, "Hullo?"

"Cristine?"

"Uh-huh."

"This is Frank Segal and I've called too early. I'm sorry."

"What? Who?"

Disappointment slapped me down. I must have hoped she'd been waiting for me to call. "Frank Segal," I repeated. "We met last week windsurfing."

"Oh. Oh! Hi." Her voice brightened. "Good morning."

"Do you remember me?"

"Of course. So funny, I thought you said Hank Eagle."

I remembered shouting my name after her as she sailed away. I laughed. "You couldn't believe a name like that?"

"What do I know? Maybe you're part Cherokee."

I laughed again. It felt good, damn good. "Listen, I'm sorry I called so early."

"What time is it...oh good lord, it isn't early. And I'm not usually this lazy."

"I just thought, I was hoping we might get together sometime this weekend if you're free."

"What exactly did you have in mind, not Hank Eagle?"

"I don't know. It depends upon whether your days or your nights are free. I...I don't mean that the way it sounded. I mean we could just, you know, I don't know, get to know each other. I mean...it doesn't really matter to me what we do."

There was a giggle on her end of the line. "Why are you nervous? I told you to call me and I'd like to get to know you, too. Tell you what, bring your board and be here at eleven. We'll take it from there."

It was a great Saturday. She had her board rigged to carry a small ice chest, which she had packed with sandwiches, drinks, cheese, and a bottle of wine. We crossed the bay to a sandbar, dry at half-tide, and lounged for hours on our own private beach. Her eyes were a translucent green, like the water all around us, and several times when she was talking, I found myself drowning in them.

She told me all about herself, her mid-western family, her college days, the job with Pan Am that brought her to Miami, about her roommate, her boss, and a couple of discarded boyfriends. She was wide open, and it made me want to tell her all about myself as well, but I couldn't. I told her what I did, where I lived, how long I had been divorced – name, rank, and serial number.

When our island disappeared beneath the flooding tide, we traded boards and raced back across the bay. On my board, she streaked out in front of me in the afternoon breeze, periodically stopping to let me catch up. I complained about the extra weight of the ice chest, but she just laughed and zoomed off again.

We sat on the seawall and watched the puffy white clouds out over the Gulf Stream turn vivid pink then soft gray as the sun went down behind us. A growl came out of the darkness.

"Good lord," she said, taking my hand and standing up. "We need something to eat. Come on."

Her apartment had a magnificent view of the bay. While I sat at the breakfast bar and watched, she did mysterious things with pots and spoons and little glass bottles, and the room began to take on a wonderful aroma. She wore a mint terry swim jacket and she caught me watching her more than once.

She was stirring something in a pot (and something on a stool if I'm honest) when she picked up one of her little bottles and looked at it more closely. "Good lord. We're out of oregano." She made a futile search through a cabinet. I volunteered to go to the market, but she said no. "Rosie will have some. Here, keep stirring this." She put the spoon in my hand. "Always in the same direction," and she was gone.

I circled the pan with the spoon conscientiously until she returned a minute later. She put the borrowed bottle on the counter and relieved me of the spoon. "That Rosie has every spice known to man."

"Salt, pepper, and cinnamon," I offered.

"Make that known to woman. She had marjoram and mace and something called cardamom. I don't even know what that is."

"I can tell you about Mace."

She threw me a pained look.

The food more than lived up to the promise the smells had made. When we had finished, she brought coffee out to the balcony where we sat side-by-side in the dark and watched the navigation lights on the bay flash on and off with distinct rhythm.

I couldn't really see her in the dark, was not looking toward her, but I knew that she was there; I could sense it, feel it, was warmed by it. A meteor perished in a long blazing arc across the southeastern sky. "Look!"

"Mmm."

I reached across the space between the chairs and found her hand. Her chair creaked and I knew that she had turned her head to face me.

After a few long minutes, I broke the silence. "What are

you thinking?"

"That you don't seem much like a police officer."

"Why not?"

"I don't know. It seems like a violent occupation."

"Not very often."

"Do you like what you do?" It was an honest question, not an accusation.

"Sometimes I like it very much."

"But not right now?"

"What makes you think that?"

"Your personality wears unhappiness like a red jacket."

I thought about that. "Do you remember when you were 13?"

"Sure."

"Were you happy then?"

"Who isn't happy at that age?"

"Last week I was blowing air into the lungs of a beautiful 13-year-old girl who had wrapped her mother's robe tightly around herself and stepped off into the deep end of the swimming pool."

"Good lord!"

"I'm sorry."

"For what?"

"For bringing that up. This has been a perfect day, at least for me. I don't want to spoil it."

She squeezed my hand. "I've enjoyed the day, too." There was a pause, a hesitation. "How you feel is who you are, and I'm interested in knowing who you are. If you can...and if you want to, I'd like to hear about her."

"Who?"

"The 13-year-old."

"There are two," I said automatically, and regretting it.

"Tell me about them."

I wanted to. Desperately. "It's an active investigation. I really can't discuss it," I said, lamely.

"Don't tell me their names."

"The one was reacting to the murder of her mother. Her attempt to die failed, but only by the narrowest margin. I might end up arresting her father for the murder."

"God."

"The father of the other one was killed because of his criminal activity. The daughter idolized him until she overheard a tape of him bragging about killing a woman. She now hates his memory. He wasn't a Sunday School teacher, but he wasn't a murderer either. Whatever he was, it wasn't her fault."

"Why would he confess?"

"It is a long, involved story. Two weeks ago, tragedy to these two girls meant seeing a boy they liked talking to another girl or getting caught wearing eye shadow. Now..." I shook my head unseen in the dark, unwilling to continue.

Neither of us spoke for a long time. I had spoiled the evening, even any chance for a relationship that we might have had. No one needs that kind of downer dumped on them.

"I was raped when I was 17." Her voice was hoarse, strained, and barely audible, but I reacted as though she had shouted at me.

"It was my uncle," she continued, "my dad's brother. He didn't hurt me, not physically anyway. He was married with three kids and his wife was pregnant at the time. They lived near the college I had selected, and they had invited me to live with them while I went to school. I'd been there for three weeks.

"After it happened, there was a terrific temptation to just keep quiet. For one thing, my folks had already had problems with me and boys." She let out a one-syllable laugh. "That's why they were so keen on my staying with my uncle. I was afraid that if they knew, they might think I was at fault. And I could just imagine what this was going to do to the families involved. But I did know right from wrong, and what he had done to me was wrong. I went straight to the police. It destroyed his family and strained my own for a terribly long time. I've often wondered since if I did the right thing, but I can never know what the outcome would've been if I had been silent. It's what I did, and that's it."

I stared at the shadow of her profile for a long time, hating a man I didn't know for what he had done to her, for what he had done to his own family.

As though she were reading my mind, she added a footnote. "His oldest daughter was 12."

It was not absolution, but it helped.

We sat quietly for a while, then soon found ourselves engaged in a more upbeat conversation. There was a lot of quiet laughter, a lot of leaning against each other's shoulders. I often found myself with my eyes closed, listening closely to every nuance of her voice as she shared with me a part of her life. A contentment that I had never experienced enveloped me, and it was a shock when I opened my eyes to see the eastern sky turning gray.

"That is dawn!"

"Mmm." She had her head on my right shoulder, her left hand entwined in my right, her right hand tucked under my arm above the elbow.

"Cristine. The sun is coming up."

She opened an eye. "Good lord!"

That got a laugh from me. "It's well past time for me to go home."

We were both stiff, each pretending not to be as we peeled ourselves loose from the vinyl straps of the lounge chairs. We crossed through the silent apartment and out the front door. She walked with me down to my car, her arm tucked into mine.

I fumbled with the keys before I finally got the door open, my tired eyes refusing to focus. The dome light illuminated the interior of the car.

"What's that?"

I looked where she pointed. "A change of clothes." The reflected light from the car caught a raised eyebrow. I misinterpreted it. "It's not what you're thinking. I thought we might go out after windsurfing."

"That wasn't what I was thinking."

"Good."

"What I *was* thinking is that the way your eyes look, it cannot be safe for you to drive home. And with a change of clothes already here, I can't think of one reason you should."

19

MONDAY, MORNING

IT WAS 6:00 A.M. MONDAY MORNING when I left her apartment. Our first date had lasted 43 hours. It seemed like a good sign.

I whistled my way through a hot shower and picked my gray suit. I selected a different tie than the one I usually wear with it, something a little jauntier.

I stopped by Benny's for a light breakfast. The food somehow didn't seem as good to me as usual, not as good as the midday breakfast Cristine had prepared for us on Sunday.

I kept remembering the texture of her skin, the depth of her green eyes. I looked around for a telephone, vaguely thinking of calling her. Perhaps she had not yet left for work.... *Whoa, whoa, whoa, you just met this girl*, I told myself. *Take it slow. Right*, I said. *I'll wait until tonight to call her.*

I left my money on the counter and, pushing Cristine into a quiet, comfortable corner of my mind, I pointed the car toward the station. Halfway there, I changed my mind and made a right at Milam-Dairy, circled the end of the runway, and eventually wound up on the Trail headed east. It was only 8:30 when I got into Coral Gables, and I knew Clarke wouldn't be there until closer to 9:00. Instead, I went left off of Le Jeune. There was an empty parking space right in front of the police station.

As I had suspected, Freeman was already in.

"What's up?" he asked when he saw me.

"I'm going to have another talk with Clarke."

"About Steiner?"

"No. About Mrs. Clarke. But I'm going to tell him that Steiner didn't kill her. I don't know how he's going to react to that, particularly if he executed Steiner. I wanted to give you the opportunity to be there."

"You think he's going to confess?"

"To Steiner's murder? No. Never. Clarke told me once that they had also tied a block to his company. That may be reason enough in his mind to justify whatever happened, murder or not."

"But you want me there?"

"It's up to you. I just didn't want you to think I was pursuing this Steiner thing behind your back."

"Look, Segal, at this point we consider the Steiner death justifiable homicide. We won't be doing any more investigation of it. Wait here."

He left me for a few minutes and returned with a file. Flipping through it, he pulled out a sheet and handed it to me. "Read that."

It began, "Detective Frank Segal, Metro Homicide, has suggested another possible scenario, strengthened by the finding that the victim was left-handed." It was my theory on the way Steiner had died, almost word for word the way I had described it to Freeman. Following it was Freeman's rebuttal.

"I put all that in the report so if something should turn up later, we will recall that we knew at the time that there was more than one way this might have gone down. But the fact is we already have all the evidence there is. Christ, you were right there when it happened. And nothing we have tells us with certainty exactly what did happen. That means we have no choice but to go with the presumption of innocence. If he did it, he got away with it."

I exhaled. "That may be word for word what the ASA told me. So, there's no reason for you to come with me to talk with Clarke and no reason for me to be concerned about stepping on toes."

"That's the way I see it," he agreed.

The sky was black when I went back out to my car. Roberts & Wilson was only a half-dozen blocks away, but before I got there a thunderstorm roared in, raining with such force that it was almost impossible to see the car directly in front of me. It was a relief when I pulled into a parking space and waited for the worst to move on. When the rain slowed, I looked up at the building that housed Roberts & Wilson and was stunned to find that I could see into the offices.

I left the car, went into the building directly across the street, and rode up to the 12th floor. The offices on the street side of the building housed two attorneys and the sales force of a copier manufacturer. I picked the copier company and went in. The receptionist was very accommodating and led me into an unoccupied office.

Across the street I could see clearly that Roger Clarke was not in his office yet. As I watched, Carmen del Portillo entered the office. She was wearing the same red dress that I had first seen her in. She had mail in her hand.

Perhaps someone in this building had seen what had happened, could confirm or refute Clarke's story. As I stood weighing the possibilities and watching Carmen place items on Roger's desk, the trailing edge of the storm moved across. The sky brightened and Carmen del Portillo faded away. The window into Clarke's office turned into a shiny silver mirror. Tuesday had been a bright day. I turned away from the glass, unsure of whether I was disappointed or relieved. I thanked the receptionist and crossed the street to the building I could no longer see into.

Carmen seemed genuinely glad to see me, flashing me a bright smile as I came around the corner. I had not seen her or Clarke since the day of the shooting. "How have you been?" I asked.

"Pretty good."

I suddenly remembered the way she had removed herself from between Boggs and me, how she had followed every instruction. "I didn't get a chance to tell you last week, but you were spectacular when everything was happening."

"Thank you. I really don't know how I did anything. I was frightened to death."

"Me, too."

She cocked her head a little, as though that possibility had not occurred to her, then she nodded.

"Any nightmares?" I asked.

Her surprise was slight, then a smile. "The first three nights," she said.

"About him or about you?"

"Him."

I thought again that he didn't deserve her, but I said it in a different way. "If you ever change your mind about him, you already know where I live." I put on my most winning smile.

She smiled back and said, "I'll keep that in mind." Then her countenance changed, the momentary gaiety in her dark eyes replaced with sincerity, pleading almost. "He's not at all like you think he is." Looking away, she added, "Life is complicated isn't it?"

Perhaps she was right. Perhaps I was looking for bad in Roger Clarke. Would my own motives bear scrutiny? I thought about his house, his business, his success. The office in his home that I found perfect. The Jaguar in the drive, the same model and color that I might have chosen. My own attraction to this woman who was so desperately in love with him. And Cheri. Beautiful and tragic Cheri. *I* gave her life, it was *my* breath she breathed, yet it was Clarke who would always get to be her father.

"Very complicated," I agreed.

"He should be in soon," she told me, and brought me a cup of fresh coffee while I waited.

The wait was not long, and Clarke waved me into his office as he went in himself. His eyes had the look of someone who had not slept well for a while. I wondered how much drinking he might be doing.

"Good morning, Frank," he said.

I guess with what we had been through together, "Detective Segal" would have seemed inappropriate. Either I had put him into a situation that almost got him killed, or he had manipulated me into helping him get away with Old Testament justice, either way I could see solid justification for a feeling that I was undeserving of any special deference.

We passed a few pleasantries while he thumbed through his mail, picking out a couple of pieces that were more pressing and laying the rest aside. I watched him, studied him, trying to fathom the man. He looked up, read my face. "What?"

"Herb Steiner didn't kill Mary."

"What!"

"Steiner did not kill Mary," I repeated, spacing between each word.

"What are you talking about? Of course, he killed her. He confessed. You've got it on tape, for Chrissake."

"He was lying."

"Are you crazy?"

"He wanted you to cooperate, to launder the cash for him. Someone told him if you were afraid of him, you wouldn't cause any more problems." I harumphed at the irony of that last sentence. "So, he let you think he was responsible for the murder."

"No! He killed her. And he would have killed Cheri, too."

I could think of a whole list of reasons why Clarke might want to argue the point with me. He either wanted to believe that Steiner had been the murderer, or he wanted me to believe it. I tried to make it clear that he was wasting his time on me. "No, he didn't. And he was just as certainly no threat to Cheri."

"But…." Clarke stopped and tried to get himself back under control. "Are you sure?"

There was a new urgency to his question. The big man was suddenly frightened, not a reaction that I had expected. Was it something he thought I knew?

"Positive," I said.

"Shit, Frank. I brought the kids back this weekend. They're at home." He was already up and headed for the door before I realized what he was thinking.

"Wait a minute, Roger. They're okay. Steiner wasn't working for anyone else, not in that sense. Cheri has never been in any danger that we're aware of."

"Aware of? What the hell does that mean?"

"Only that we weren't aware, ahead of time, of any danger to Mary either. Steiner had nothing to do with her death and was never a threat to Cheri. His was a bluff – that's all. I'm not as certain that an associate of his had nothing to do with Mary's death, but it seems a very remote possibility to me. In any case, Cheri isn't likely to be in danger from that quarter.

"But listen up, Roger. If you are involved in something else that you haven't told me about, something that somehow resulted in the murder of your wife, then Cheri could be in a great deal of danger."

"Something else?" He came back to his chair and sat down.

"Someone with a grudge against you. Someone whose money you lost, someone you fired...." I stopped. He had fired three officers, Chip Harris and two others whose names were in my case notes, only a couple of weeks before Mary's disappearance.

"Steiner has to be involved. He has to be!" Clarke declared. I was going forward but his mind was going in reverse.

"Why?" I asked.

"He said he did it. He said it with such...such...hatred."

"You called him a sideshow freak, a midget, not a real person." I knew the taped exchange by heart. "The hatred was for you, for what you were saying to him, for your disdain."

"He was going to kill me," he said.

I still couldn't tell whether he was talking to me or to himself I wanted to accuse him, to tell him what I thought had happened in this office last Tuesday, but I didn't. Carmen had planted seeds of doubt about my opinion of Clarke. Besides, there was no way that I could prove my accusations. Most of all, I was working on the Clarke death, not Steiner's, and alienating Roger Clarke would not help that. I decided to let him create his own private hell if he had executed Steiner. Judge Segal sentences you to life.

"I don't think so. Steiner was just a little guy looking for respect and a better life for his family – like the rest of us, I guess, except that he was going about it all wrong, misdirected by an incredibly poor choice of friends. The tragedy is the gutted wife he had been married to for 17 years and still wrote poetry for, the small boy who won't remember his daddy, and the daughter – about Cheri's age – who will never forgive him."

Clarke turned green, a bilious yellow-green, and his eyes lost their focus. The enormity of taking another man's life finally came crashing through the barriers of justification and rationalization that he had erected.

I offered him a full pardon; he would take it if he deserved it. "But listen, Roger. Don't be too hard on yourself. You couldn't be expected to think anything other than what you did when Steiner pulled his gun. That your shot was so deadly was just a tragic stroke of bad luck."

He didn't speak for a long time, staring beyond me, seeing, I was sure, a scene in his mind that I had only heard.

I gave him time, suggested coffee which he called for like an automaton, and waited. After a while he rejoined me, but his perspective on life had been altered.

"Tell me about Chip Harris," I said finally.

"What?"

"And the other two officers you fired."

"Why?"

"Steiner didn't kill Mary. That means someone else did."

"Chip?"

"Maybe?" It was more of a question.

"No. Chip worked for me for 14 years. He couldn't do anything like that."

"Drugs cause people to do things that even they can't believe. Did you expect his involvement in this laundering scheme?"

"I just can't believe that Chip would hurt anyone." He was trying to convince himself. I made a note to have a talk with Mr. Chip Harris.

"What about the other two?"

"Raul and Dan? No. They would have no reason."

"You fired them!"

"They weren't involved with Chip, but they knew what he was doing, suspected anyway, and they failed to tell me. I wanted a clean staff, squeaky clean. If this ever came out, I wanted to be able to say that I got rid of everyone who even had knowledge that it occurred."

"All the more reason for those two to be especially bitter," I pointed out.

"No. I had trouble with their punishment being as harsh as Chip's. Three days after I fired them, I called the president of a company like ours downtown and got him to hire them both, with a substantial increase in their earnings, so it would look as though they had made the move for economic reasons."

"Do they know you did that?"

"Sure. I called them and sent them for the interviews."

I made a couple of notes, let him watch me flip through the notebook, put a little time between the last subject and the one I was about to raise. I stopped at the page I was looking for. "Some time ago, I asked you a question which you at first refused to answer. When I pressed you on it, you lied."

His face told me that he had no idea what I was talking about.

"On the day that Mary disappeared, I want to know where you were between 1:30 and 3:00 in the afternoon."

"What did I tell you?" He had a look that I hadn't seen before. Puzzlement, maybe.

"You told me you were in your office."

"But you know I wasn't."

"Where were you?"

"You already know. You told me that everyone knew."

"I want to know exactly where you were. When you left, when you got back? Who was with you? Who saw you?"

He was becoming visibly agitated, angry, red of face. "Why are you doing this? Is this some kind of voyeuristic kick for you?"

"What?" Now I was the one puzzled.

"You know I was with Carmen." It was a denunciation, not a simple statement of fact.

"Where?"

"In the condo."

"Did anyone else see you?"

"No. Not that we were aware of. Maybe whoever told you." He spat the words.

"Will Carmen confirm this?"

"Do you have to bring her into this?"

"Yes. Why don't I just talk with her right now and get it

over with?"

"Couldn't you just…shit, okay."

Carmen and I went into Chip Harris' vacant office. She told me that on that Tuesday, she and Roger had gone out together to lunch. She told me the name of the restaurant, that Roger had paid with American Express.

The condo that Roger had mentioned was only two buildings away from Roberts & Wilson. It belonged to the company and was used in place of a hotel for out-of-town clients. Roger brought the key and they went there from the restaurant, parking in the garage and taking the residents' elevator up. She made it clear that this was not something that they did often.

No one had seen them come or go. She called housekeeping after they returned to the office and asked for the unit to be serviced with fresh linens. She said there should be a record of that because they were charged for housekeeping services.

It occurred to me that Roger might have been using her as an alibi while someone he had hired was murdering his wife. But being in bed with the "other woman" would cast suspicion on him, hardly a good selection of an alibi – unless he was very, very clever. Roger Clarke was not that clever.

Carmen wanted to know what difference any of this made now. I took now to mean now that someone had confessed. I told her the truth about Steiner. Her quick mind immediately grasped all that implied.

I still didn't understand his ire at being asked about this event and I said as much to Carmen.

"Guilt," she said.

I shook my head, indicating that I still didn't understand.

"We haven't been together, he and I, since that afternoon. When he realized where he was, what he was doing, while his wife was enduring whatever horrors he has conjured up in his mind, he was overcome with guilt."

I must have looked dubious because she said, "You still think he might be the one you're looking for. You're wrong. Roger never blamed Mary for their problems, for his problems. He blamed himself. He thought he had the perfect family, that Mary was the perfect wife and mother. He couldn't understand why he wasn't happy."

She was running her thumb back and forth on the edge of the chair arm. Tears suddenly began to roll down her cheeks. "He's such an idiot. He doesn't even realize that it was because he didn't love her. He thinks he didn't deserve her. He blames himself – and it's just a matter of time before he blames me, too."

I thought that she would be better off without him, but she was in such obvious distress that I said, "Maybe not," hoping to comfort her.

I was sure that the jerk had sold her a bill of goods. Go to bed with me, get involved with me, but don't expect too much because I already have a wife – a perfect wife. *But wait a minute!* A harsh, white light came on inside my head. If that was true, it disqualified Clarke from contention for "murderer of the week."

I looked at the woman in front of me, dabbing her eyes with a tissue, and I could not convince myself that she might be lying. Maybe she just didn't know Roger as well as she thought she did. Maybe he had been trying to avoid *her* suspicion. But if he's planning to kill his wife and trying to avoid suspicion, why does he get involved with another woman at all? I wondered if

I still had that bottle of aspirin in the car.

When I got back to Clarke's office, he was standing in front of the glass wall, looking out. His shoulders were so slumped that it made his suit jacket look too large for him. If, in fact, Mary's death had been a bolt out of the blue, whoever was responsible had dragged Roger Clarke's life over rough terrain.

"Roger?"

He turned slowly to face me, hard to see against the brilliance of the Florida sunlight behind him. I realized that the jacket was too large. "I'm leaving," I told him.

He nodded.

Before I got back through the door, he stopped me. "Frank."

I waited.

"Steiner's family. Do they need any assistance? Financial… counseling…I don't know. They wouldn't have to know where it was coming from."

"I'll find out."

"Thanks."

20

MONDAY, MIDDAY

THE GARAGE DOOR WAS CLOSED when I wheeled up into the empty driveway. It occurred to me that I should have called. As I stepped out of the air-conditioned car into the humid heat, my sunglasses fogged over. I had reached back into the car to lay them on the seat when I heard a scream and a crash come from inside the house. I dropped instinctively into a crouch, acutely aware that part of my legs was completely exposed beneath the car door.

I stayed there for a long minute, the midday sun trying to fry my brain, sweat running down the knobs of my spine. No other sounds came from the house. With considerable trepidation, I gave up the semi-security of the car door, moving quickly and quietly to the front of the garage.

It was still quiet in the house. I slipped through the bushes and onto the porch, flattened against the wall beside the window. Silence. Two deep breaths and I pitched my precious and vulnerable head out in front of the window for a quick look inside, drawing back like a startled turtle. Wanda was there, sitting on the sofa in the family room.

I took a longer look, but nothing was happening. Crossing quickly in front of the window, I rang the bell. She came into the living room alone. Seeing me through the window, she made various clicks and rattles as she unlocked and unlatched the door.

Wanda Steiner looked like she had been in a car accident. The swelling had gone, but the right side of her face was a painful looking mix of yellow and purple. Her eyes were red and puffy, the tracks of her tears showing clearly on the unbruised side of her face.

"If I've come at a bad time...?"

The look she flashed me made me feel like an insensitive clod. When did I expect the good times to start?

"It's okay. Come in."

The sweat was still leaking past the band of my Jockey shorts. "Is someone here?"

She didn't notice my nervousness. "Just Helen."

I replayed the crash. A slammed door. A daughter still angry at her father's betrayal.

I followed her through the immaculate living room into the equally spotless family room and accepted her offer for a soda. She took her time in the kitchen, gathering herself back together, I supposed. When she came back, I told her that Boggs was going to jail.

"What about Arturo?"

"Not yet."

"I see." I was sure that she did.

I placed the tape cassette that I brought on the shining coffee table.

"What's that?"

"A copy of your phone messages tape. Can you listen to the messages on either side of Ribera's and give me an idea when Herb got the call?"

"I don't need to do that. It was about 6:30 on Monday evening."

"How do you know that?"

"Because Monday was the night we went out to the movies. It was a weekly family event." Was! The verb ripped away at my gut. "While Herb was talking to Arturo, Helen kept whispering, 'Come on. It starts at 7:00.' We got there in time, so the call must have been around 6:30."

I mentally scratched Arturo Ribera's name from my dwindling list of suspects.

"I don't know yet how to take Ribera off the street, but I do know how you can hurt him a great deal if you want to."

"How?"

"He might retaliate. You might be placing yourself, even your kids, in danger."

"How?" she asked again. The voice was cold, the decision made.

"Sometime this week a reporter, a columnist really, will come to see you. He'll be looking for a human-interest story – the drug-business-induced devastation of a happy, middle-class family. Tell him your story, all of it, from the dreams of high-school sweethearts to the reality of now. And tell him about a friend snaring Herb into the drug business, the price he paid...the price you've all paid. Name the friend. Newspapers do not much like to be sued, so give the writer this tape."

"How will that hurt Arturo?"

"It's better if you don't know. Your purpose in telling the story is to prevent other families from falling into the same trap, not vengeance. That's important. And please don't mention me."

The high-pitched scream of a motorcycle engine wound to

its limit interrupted our conversation. When the bike reached the house, there was the bark of rubber against asphalt as the rider braked hard. Reflected sunlight ran across the ceiling and the back wall of the room. The growling engine went silent.

From somewhere else in the house, another door slammed. Helen Steiner, looking a petite 18, came into the room. She was wearing a thin, white midriff blouse and very tight black shorts. Her lips were painted a bright red, her eyes shadowed with a shade of purple like her mother's bruised face. Mascara swept out of the corners of her eyes in little up-turned duck tails. Except for the flat shoes, she could have been on her way to work a corner on 79th Street.

She and her mother exchanged looks that sent chills through me. Without any acknowledgment of my presence in the room, without a single utterance to her mother, she went through the living room and out the front door. The motorcycle rumbled back to life and for a minute or more we could hear it as the rider accelerated away from the stop signs in the neighborhood.

I didn't see the motorcycle rider, but I imagined the worst. Even if he was the class president, it had to be a class at least three or four years beyond Helen's. She shouldn't have gone out looking like that, shouldn't be sitting behind some kid on a motorcycle, and damn sure shouldn't be out with some high-school Harry with only one thought on his mind.

But I kept my opinions to myself. Parents rarely appreciate criticism from those of us who are not. Besides, if there's one thing I know nothing about, it's kids.

"You're right," Wanda said.

"About?"

"What you were thinking. What kind of mother lets her 13-year-old daughter go out with a 17-year-old boy? And looking like that!"

I wondered if I was that transparent, or had we reacted the same because of the stimulus, like "ouch" to a burn.

"That wasn't what I was thinking."

"I don't know what to do," she said, ignoring my denial. "Just before you came, we had another terrible fight. I'm afraid to push her too far. She's already told me that she'll run away, and right now I believe her. I'm just trying to hold us together until the pain dulls a little."

"I put them in the room together."

"What?"

"Herb and Roger Clarke. I was the one that got them together in the same room. I should have expected what happened, but I didn't."

She stared at me, not comprehending. "Why are you telling me this?"

"I don't know," I said. And I didn't.

21

MONDAY, AFTERNOON

WHEN I GOT BACK TO THE STATION, I made a telephone call to a friend at the *Herald*. He agreed to interview Wanda. Then I found an empty conference room and spread out the Clarke file. I reread every report, looked at every note, re-examined every photograph. I reconsidered everyone that I had considered even remotely a suspect. And I came up empty.

I was out of suspects and out of leads. There was still Chip Harris to check out, but despite my justification to Roger Clarke, I could see little reason for Harris to harm Mary Clarke. I stared at the blank wall. Somewhere out there, beyond that wall, the person or persons that did kill Mary Clarke were still walking around, business as usual. And they were going to get away with it because one Detective Frank Segal was too blind or too stupid to see the tracks left behind. My mind railed in protest. It was not the first time I had failed to solve a case, but an abscessed tooth isn't any less painful just because you've had one before. If anything, the anticipation makes it that much worse.

Out of frustration, I packed up and signed out for the day. When I got home, the rack was still on the top of my car. Why not, I thought. I changed clothes, loaded the board, and 20 minutes later was paying the attendant at the toll booth at the entrance to Rickenbacker Causeway. The beaches on either side of the causeway are packed with cars, vans, and trailers on weekends, but on a Monday afternoon they are virtually empty. I pulled off the causeway and drove along the drive behind the beach, looking for the best spot.

I parked between two large pines and walked down to the water's edge, inhaling deeply the sharp smell of the seawater. To my right a lone catamaran sat on the beach, its colorful sail waving in the light breeze. Far down the beach to my left, almost to the water, sat a white and red motorcycle, sparkling in the afternoon sun. On the seat sat a small girl in black shorts and a white top, her elbows locked around her knees.

It seemed unlikely to me at first. But the shore of Biscayne Bay is owned by the wealthy. If a heartbroken little girl wanted to sit at the water's edge and let the rippled reflections wash over her mind, there were only three likely spots. This was one of them.

I backed out and drove farther down the beach, parking close to the bike. It was Helen, all right, but I didn't see the boy she was with. I didn't look her way but got busy unloading the board, slipping the mast into the sleeve of the sail, rigging the wishbone, and getting everything into the water. I had my doubts about whether she would recognize me anyway in a red and green bathing suit instead of a suit and tie.

I always underestimate kids. When I looked up from snapping the mast in place, she was standing in front of the board.

"Did my mom send you?"

"Excuse me?"

"I know who you are."

I thought of about three ways to play it, but I decided to just play it straight. "I know who you are, too. And no, your mother didn't send me. I'm here to do this." I patted the board.

"Sure."

"Okay." I pushed the board out into waist-deep water and hopped up on it. The sail came up easily in the light breeze. We stared at each other from a short distance for a minute; she wondering what the hell I *was* doing here and me wondering what the hell I *could* do here. I nodded toward the motorcycle. "Make him be careful on that thing. You're too pretty to spend the rest of your life all scarred up."

The wind was too light for my weight and I drifted back to the beach in about 20 minutes. She was still there and her friend was under a tree, sitting on his helmet football player style. No tattoos, no earrings, no leather or spikes; he looked a lot like one of the kids that shot hoops on my street.

She walked down to the water to meet me. "Back so soon?"

I ignored her sarcastic tone. "Yeah. The wind's too light for me with this sail. It would be good for someone like you."

There was a flicker of interest.

"You ever try it?" I asked.

"No."

The motorcycle jockey had deserted his helmet and come to find out what was going on.

"You want to try it? The wind's perfect for learning."

"No," she said.

I looked at the boy. He was giving the board a critical appraisal. "You sail?" I asked him.

"Yeah."

"Help yourself."

"Hey, thanks!" He kicked off his sneakers, dropped his shirt on top of them, and pushed the board out into deeper water.

Helen went back to the motorcycle seat. I got a beach chair, a canvas hat, and a small cooler out of my trunk and sat with my feet in the water.

Her friend wasn't very good. In the light wind, he could only get the board to go in one direction. When he tried to come back, he kept letting the wind get on the wrong side of the sail, pitching him into the water time after time. Finally, he swam the board ashore and walked back to where we were. Helen was there when he beached the board. "Wind's too light," he said.

"Um-hum."

She was razzing him, but he refused the fight. "Try it."

"No."

"Okay. I'm going to run again, then we'll go."

After he jogged away down the beach, she stood for a long time looking at the beached board, its floating multicolored Dacron sail. "It's pretty," she said. "The sail."

"Yeah. I have another one, a bigger one, that's spectacular. That's the one I should have brought."

She turned around to look at my shadowed face. "My mom really didn't send you?"

"Does she even know where you are?"

"I guess not." She looked back toward the board. "Is it hard to learn?"

"Boardsailing?"

"Yeah. I don't know anything about sailing."

"It's easy. I could teach you in an hour."

"I don't have my bathing suit."

"You are going to be on the board, not in the water. If you do fall, will a little water hurt what you have on?"

"I guess not."

She was a natural athlete and she listened with surprising intensity to everything I told her. By the time her friend came huffing back up the beach, she was sailing back and forth just off the beach.

"Hey, all right!" he encouraged her. "Lookin' good."

I yelled an occasional instruction about spreading her hands, or moving her feet, or keeping her back straight. As she came by us on one pass, she caught an unexpected gust. "Lean into it! Lean into it!" I shouted. With her light weight, the board shot forward, kicking up a rooster tail at the stern. The lull caught her still leaning and the unsupported sail came right over on top of her.

When she popped to the surface, sputtering and coughing, her face was glowing with excitement. "Wow!"

"On a good day, you can go like that for hours," I told her.

She was already back on the board when her friend said, "Helen, we gotta go. I gotta be at work at 5:00."

"Oh." She pulled the board to the beach, looking like a little kid who had just been told it was time to get out of the pool.

"If you want to stay and sail, I'll take you home," I offered

Her eyes lit up. "Mark, would you mind?"

"Are you crazy? You don't know this guy."

She hadn't told him.

"Yes, she does," I said. "I'm a family friend."

She gave me a quizzical look. "He's a cop, Mark. My mom knows him. It'll be okay, I don't want to go home yet."

He didn't much like it, but he agreed. He also agreed to call

Wanda and tell her that Helen was with me.

She sailed until almost 7:00, improving hourly and several times asking me if I wanted to sail, but the wind remained weak. In fading light, we loaded the board onto the car. I stopped at a waterside burger spot in Coconut Grove to call Wanda to confirm Mark had called her, catching Helen studying the menu board. So, I placed an order and we sat at a plywood table on the seawall while I had a dolphin sandwich and Helen devoured a burger and both orders of fries.

The waters of the bay had removed all the makeup, exposing an innocent 13-year-old who kept measuring the distance between her hands, practicing her grip as it would be on the sailboard's wishbone. I wanted to talk to her about her father, to try to rectify some of the damage, but I was sure she would just shut me out. So, I let her lead the conversation and it mostly hovered around windsurfing.

I waited until we were on her street before I risked losing her by saying, "You know, your mom is hurting as much as you are. She needs your help, not your anger."

There was no response. When I pulled into the driveway, I expected her to bolt from the car, but she sat without moving while I turned off the engine. I waited.

"I...I...had fun. Thanks." Then she was out of the car.

I opened my door. "Helen?"

She stopped on the walkway, but she didn't look toward me.

"We'll sail again. Soon."

"Sure."

As I backed out of the drive, Wanda was letting her in.

* * *

I tried Cristine from the first telephone booth I found, but there was no answer, so I drove on home. The only thing on television was a police show, and I watched with detached interest as the homicide detective figured it all out just in time to save the beautiful girl from becoming the next victim, meting out justice with a perfect shot from two hundred yards. Neither the murderer nor the victims had families.

It was too hot to sleep without the air conditioner, and the drone of the unit soon put me under. I woke up before the alarm went off and stared at the ceiling until the buzzer sounded. The bed linens looked as though I had lost a very tough wrestling match.

I had breakfast at Benny's, then drove to the station where I played 20 questions with Wayne about his latest case. About 10:00 I called Carmen and got Chip Harris' address. Then she put me through to Roger Clarke, and I told him what I wanted. He agreed immediately and gave me a credit card number over the telephone. I spent the rest of the day bringing the file up to date in anticipation of moving on to another case. Around two I drove down U.S. 1 to the sailboard shop I frequented. The owner was a tan, sun-bleached hunk, twice state champion in competition boardsailing. I told him I wanted a board that would stretch her, and he helped me with the selection. We added an additional sail and a car-top rack to the charge receipt. He helped me mount the rack on the cruiser and load the board.

Helen wasn't home but I left the board and rack with Wanda

"What's this?"

"It's for Helen. She discovered yesterday that she can still have fun. Get her to the water with this as much as you can. She likes it better than motorcycles."

Wanda understood. "How did you find her?"

I shook my head. "I didn't. We just happened to be at the same place." For similar reasons, I thought. "Did she say anything?"

"Just that you were nice. Your boat?"

"No. It's hers."

"What? Oh no, no," Wanda protested. "Unh-uh. We don't…"

"Wait a minute! Listen to me. Someone gave me this board and I have another board and I don't need this one and it's not my size and it's perfect for Helen. I swear I didn't spend a cent. I want her to have it."

Her wide-set eyes caught me in their gaze as she tried to see what was happening deep in my soul. She must have seen something because her hard, bruised face softened. She looked back at the gaily striped board. "You think I could learn to do this?"

"I don't know. Ask Helen."

*   *   *

The address Carmen had given to me for Chip Harris was less than a mile from the Steiner home. I had considered waiting to interview him until Vice brought him in on the laundering charges, but it might be weeks before that happened. I was this close, and I wanted to tie up all the loose ends on Mary Clarke's murder and move on, so I decided to have a conversation with him now.

A boy of about 15 opened the door. He was Chip Harris, Jr. After I showed him my badge, he told me that his mother was at work and his father was away.

"Away, where?"

"Why?"

I wondered what happened to more innocent times when kids viewed police officers with implicit trust. Today it was always suspicion. "I would like to talk to him."

"About what?"

I was not at all interested in continuing this exchange. "Look, son, does your dad have some reason to hide from the police?" It was a "Do you still beat your wife?" kind of question.

Chip, Jr. hesitated only a second. "No, of course not."

"Then there's no reason for you not to tell me where I can reach him."

"I don't have to tell you anything," he said.

"No," I said, "you don't." I gave him a hard look and a positive nod. "I'll be back."

He reconsidered and caught me at the car. "My dad's in a hospital...sort of."

The tacked-on "sort of" told me what was going on.

"In Miami?"

"No."

When he didn't continue, I asked him where.

"Maryland." He gave me the name of a well-known drug rehab center between Baltimore and Washington, D.C.

"Thanks," I said. I had gotten in the habit recently of feeling sorry for the kids and I added, "He's doing the right thing."

Chip Harris, Jr. just looked at me with troubled eyes, then turned away without comment and went back into the house.

I drove back to the station and used the WATS line to call Maryland. It took 25 minutes and three transfers to finally get to a person who would even consider telling me anything about a patient. I assured her that I did not want to know anything about Chip Harris' medical condition or the treatment he was receiving. In connection with a homicide investigation, I was merely trying to establish when he had entered the program and if he had been there constantly since that time. She told me that she would check with the director and call me back. I suggested that for her own assurance she obtain the Metro-Dade Police number from information and ask for me through the main switchboard.

While I waited for the call, I again flipped through the photographs in the file. I found myself looking at one of the last photos I had asked Charlie to take, a photo of Mary Clarke's feet tied securely to the concrete block. Something stirred in the back of my mind. The cord. The neatness of the cord. What did that tell me?

If I had just killed someone and I was going to weight them down with a block, wouldn't I be more concerned with speed than neatness? Wouldn't I be worried about someone walking in on me while I was tying her feet? The murderer had time.

But that wasn't news. Mary disappeared sometime before 3:00 in the afternoon and wasn't dropped off the bridge until the dark of the night. There was time to be neat, but why? The murderer was neat by nature? There was something there, something I couldn't quite grasp.

The woman in Maryland called me back in less than 20 minutes to give me the information I wanted. Chip Harris had entered the program eight days before Mary Clarke disappeared. He hadn't been off the premises since that day.

22

TUESDAY, EVENING

I was almost home, sitting at a signal light, spinning the dial on the radio. One of the oldies stations was playing Simon and Garfunkel, and I paused in my search for Brahms. The music dredged up a picture of Pam and me, sitting in the convertible, top down, facing the bay, her face lit only by the glow of the radio dial. We had known so little back then, assigned significance to everything, especially to the song that was playing when we reached a new plateau in our relationship. This had been one of "our" songs, only now I couldn't connect it with any specific event. I wondered if Pam could.

The light changed and the car behind me honked. As I pulled away, I found myself singing along with the radio: ". . . parsley, sage, rosemary and thyme."

Rosemary and thyme. And marjoram and mace. Cristine came breezing into my head, displacing thoughts of Pam, like the sun sweeps the morning sky clear of stars. Our first day together began to play through my mind like a feature-length movie; the sandbar island, nightfall from the seawall, stirring the pot in her fragrant kitchen waiting for her to…

"Jesus Christ!" I whipped the wheel to the right into a parking lot in front of a darkened dentist's office, stopped the car, and sat motionless while the thought matured. Marjoram and mace. And she had named another one – carda-something. Man? Mon? Mom? That was it. Cardamom. That couldn't be something her friend kept right out on the front of the shelf.

I looked quickly down the street. About two blocks ahead, on the opposite side of the street, was a convenience store. I drove there and went to one of the telephones on the outside wall. In the dim light I searched my notebook for Roger Clarke's home number and dialed it. Cheri answered on the first ring.

"Cheri, this is Frank Segal. How are you?"

"Oh," There was disappointment in her voice. She had been expecting a call from someone else. "Hi. Pretty good, thank you."

For the first time I realized that the less important I was to her, the better off she was going to be. It was a bitter pill.

"Is your father at home?"

She got him to the telephone, and I told him that I was on my way down and that I needed to talk to him and Cheri, both. He wanted to know what about and I told him I would explain when I got there.

"Is Cheri in any danger?" he asked anxiously.

I assured him it was nothing like that.

Despite the late hour, it took almost 30 minutes before I was turning off Old Cutler into the Clarkes' fine neighborhood. I passed Marsha Goodwin's house and noticed her light ivory Mercedes was sitting in the drive. I wondered how she might be planning to pay for it now that Wayne had relieved her of neighbor Stacy Walters' outrageous necklace.

Roger answered the bell and started to lead me back to his office, the one I liked so well. I stopped him.

"I need to talk with you and Cheri both. Actually, Cheri may be the one who can answer my question."

He stood in the hallway and studied my face. "She's doing well, Frank. I don't want to upset her. Nothing we can accomplish is worth a risk to her."

I couldn't blame him for wanting to protect her, but not to the extent of letting someone get away with murder. "Are you forgetting that someone killed her mother?"

His response was emotionless. "You know I'm not. But how long does the process go on? And if you do find the killer, then what? Trials and appeals? Capital punishment protests, or worse yet, parole hearings? All of that is hard enough on an adult, but on a child...? I don't want all her teenage years played out against that kind of backdrop. And in a couple of more years, Adam will understand what's going on."

He had been thinking about it – a lot, and there was truth in what he was saying. "It's not always that way," I countered. "And when it is, that's how our system works. The alternative is worse."

"No. To trade Cheri's chance for a normal life to punish some...some...whacked-out junkie...."

"Is that what you think? A junkie killed Mary?"

"Who else? If it was someone getting even with me, wouldn't they want me to know, or at least suspect, that they had made me pay? I can't think of anyone except Steiner, who you say didn't do it. Or Chip?"

"Chip left the state eight days before Mary's disappearance. Unless he hired it done, he's not involved."

"See! And Mary didn't have an enemy in the world. She was as close to perfect as they come."

"Listen, Roger, I need your help. And Cheri's. Then I'm going to put this case to bed one way or the other. I just want to know about the cake."

"The what?"

"The cake. You told me that when Mary disappeared, it was Cheri's birthday, and Mary was making a cake. When you got home, everything was on the counter just like she must have left it. Isn't that what you told me?"

"Yes, but…"

"I *need* to know about that cake. What kind of cake was it?"

Roger Clarke backed away from me one step for a wider view. "You can't be serious. Is this a trick, a decoy of some kind?"

"Get Cheri and let's go out into the kitchen. Tell me everything you can about the cake, and I'll leave. You have my word."

Clarke exhaled sharply through his nose and shook his head side to side. He turned and went down the hall to Cheri's room and knocked on the door.

The luminous ceiling cast no shadows in the cheery red and white kitchen. The three of us stood where not so long ago we would have been in the way. When I was growing up, my mother spent much of her time in the kitchen. I could not picture the kitchen of my childhood without seeing my mother there. I thought that this kitchen must seem cold and unfriendly to the small girl staring up at me.

Cheri had joined us wide-eyed, wondering what this was all about. She still looked fragile, and I understood Roger's desire to protect her.

"The day your mother disappeared," I began, wording it as gently as I could, "she was baking a cake?"

"Uh-huh."

"Do you know what kind of cake it was?"

"Sure. It was a birthday cake."

"No, that's not what I mean. I want to know what kind of cake it was, like angel food or carrot or pineap…"

"Black Forest," she said.

"Black Forest?"

"Uh-huh."

"How do you know that was what she was making?" I asked.

"Because when she took me to school, she told me that she was going to bake another kind of cake, and I asked her to make a Black Forest instead. She said she would."

Roger pulled a chair from beneath the table in the kitchen and sat down.

"What is a Black Forest cake?" I asked her.

"It's kinda like a chocolate cake, but cream filled with little chocolate squiggly thingies all over it."

"Sounds pretty good," I said.

"It's great," she agreed.

"Do you know the recipe?"

"It's in one of the cookbooks."

I waited while Cheri opened the cabinet and pulled down several cookbooks. She began opening them to the back and looking for Black Forest in the index. I glanced at Roger; I could almost hear the wheels turning as he tried to figure out what possible reason I had for wanting to see the recipe for a chocolate cake.

"Here it is." It was the third index she had examined. She flipped the book to the designated page which faced a glossy photo of a very dark and very fancy chocolate cake on a glass stand. "Yeah, this is the one she used."

I looked at the recipe. It required about a dozen different ingredients and didn't look too complicated. I turned back to Roger. "Was the cake actually started when you got here?"

"Uh…"

Cheri came to his rescue. "No. She just had all the different stuff sitting out."

"Can we do the same thing?"

Her forehead wrinkled. "What do you mean?"

"Can we get out the pans and the bowls, and all the ingredients, just like we were going to make the cake?"

She looked over at her father. He gave her a shrug. "I guess so," she said, "but we can't actually make it."

"Why not?"

"Because we don't have everything." She was looking at the book. "I don't think we have enough eggs and I know we don't have any heavy cream."

"How was your mom going to do it?"

"I guess she had everything. I know she had the cream because it was spoiled – from sitting on the counter – and I poured it out."

"Okay. Let's just see how close we can get."

While Roger and I watched, Cheri pulled out bowls, pans, boxes, and canisters. She kept checking the book and getting things out of the cabinet and the refrigerator.

"It calls for kirsch and I can't reach that. It's up there in that cabinet," she said, indicating one above the refrigerator. "We keep it up there so Adam can't reach it."

That made me look at Roger and he rolled his eyes. She was

doing her best to take over for Mary. I took down the needed bottle of kirsch.

She checked the recipe one more time, touching every item on the counter in turn. "Okay, that's everything."

"Are you missing anything?"

"Just the cream. And we only have three eggs."

Damn! It could have been the eggs, I supposed, but that wasn't what I was looking for. "Has Ms. Goodwin or your aunt done any grocery shopping?"

"Aunt Betty took me shopping once while she was here."

I swept my hand over all the ingredients arrayed on the red tile. "Do you remember if you bought any of these?"

She looked again at the items. "No."

"You don't remember?"

"No, we didn't buy any of these," she clarified.

"What about the eggs?"

"No. We don't eat eggs much and there was almost a full carton when she was here."

So, it was not the eggs, either. I turned and walked to the back door and looked out through its glass panel at the door out of the screen room. Out of the screen room. That had to be the answer. But...I could feel their eyes on the back of my neck. I turned back around, holding my left hand up under my chin.

"Well?" Roger said.

I felt my eyebrows flick up and I shook my head side to side.

"What were you looking for?" he wanted to know.

"I didn't find it," I evaded.

He had no interest in pursuing it. "Then you're through?"

"Yeah..." But I just couldn't turn it loose, couldn't escape the conviction that it was here. Maybe… "No, wait!"

"Segal, you promised…"

I held up my hand. "Five minutes. No more. Cheri, let's make this cake."

"But we don't have the cream."

"We'll just pretend," I said. "We need measuring cups and spoons, don't we?"

She looked at Roger again, but he was watching me, so she opened a drawer and took out a few items.

The recipe started with eggs, sugar, and flour. We measured out everything and, without mixing them, set them aside. Except for the eggs, everything we needed for the cake was there. Then we started on the cream filling. We skipped the spoiled quart of heavy cream. The next item was one cup of powdered sugar.

Cheri dug through the drawers again and opened cabinets. "I can't find the one-cup cup," she said.

"That's okay. We'll just fill the half-cup twice," I told her.

Cheri picked up the box and poured it into the smaller measuring cup. Before the first half-cup was full, the box was empty.

I suppressed what I was feeling. "Is there more powdered sugar in the cabinet? Another box maybe?"

She looked and I helped her. We moved every grocery item in the kitchen, but no other box of powdered sugar appeared.

We went through the rest of the ingredients, all of which were there. When we were through, I helped Cheri pour everything back. I made it a point to pour the powdered sugar back into its box myself, hefting the box afterward. It was very light. I was sure that an experienced cook would know immediately that the box didn't contain a cup of sugar. I was just as sure that the missing measuring cup, the one for the required amount of this ingredient, was no coincidence.

Roger showed me out without asking any questions, and I didn't volunteer any answers. The less he knew, the better.

23

TUESDAY, NIGHT

I backed out of clarke's driveway and drove around the corner. Her Mercedes wasn't there, but it might be in the garage. I pulled into the drive opposite of where it had been.

The night was still warm, but I noticed that the front windows were open, the big central air-conditioning unit beside the house was silent. She was home and conserving.

I saw the little glass eyeball in the center of the door go dark and then she turned on the porch light. The door opened and she stood looking at me, a comfortable smile on her freckled face. I suddenly remembered the look of apprehension she had shown the last time I had been here. The reason for that look was clear to me now, and this look told me she had gotten used to the idea that she wasn't going to get caught.

She was wearing a jumpsuit the color of the Mercedes, and with her red hair and her height, she was striking. No jury would ever recommend the death penalty, no judge ever hand down such a sentence, no matter how deserved.

"Detective Segal, hello."

"Ms. Goodwin."

"Come in, come in, before the mosquitoes join us."

I went into the beautifully furnished living room and she

motioned me into the first chair, a piece of art in carved wood and velvet. It was unexpectedly comfortable. She seated herself across from me on a long, multi-legged sofa.

"Are you here on a social call, or do you keep such late office hours?"

I glanced up at the ornate clock on the mantel and discovered that it was well after 10:00. I felt no inclination to apologize.

"I am afraid I'm here on business, Ms. Goodwin," I said.

"You're still looking for the person who killed Mary?"

"No," I replied, never taking my eyes off her face. "I found her. Tonight."

"Oh? Well that's good news, isn't it?"

"I suppose that depends upon your perspective."

Her face clouded. "What do you mean?"

"You told me you didn't see Mary Clarke on the afternoon she disappeared."

"I didn't."

I kept my eyes locked on hers. "Did she tell you why she needed the powdered sugar?" Her eyes changed, instantly filled with the fear of a trapped animal. "Did she tell you it was for a birthday cake for Cheri, or did you find that out later?"

"What are you talking about?"

"The only part I don't know is the part about the necklace. I know she would have recognized it, but how did she see it? Did you just tell her to help herself and she opened the wrong canister? Could you have been that careless?"

"I don't know what you're talking about."

"You were right to think she would have told. It's the kind of person she was. But wouldn't giving it back have made more sense than killing her?"

"You're accusing me of killing my neighbor?"

"Such a drastic step – and you got caught with the necklace anyway. What a tragic waste."

"Just because I took that necklace doesn't give you any right to accuse me of killing someone."

"You had so much time to reconsider, to come to your senses. Were you trying all that time to persuade her to keep your secret? When did you finally decide on murder?"

Her eyes told me that I had lost her.

A cold chill ran through me. "Oh, shit," I swore and looked away from her. "It wasn't that way at all, was it? You didn't *decide* to kill her. When she found the necklace, you tried to stop her from leaving, didn't you?" A picture of what must have happened was playing through my mind. "Maybe you didn't hit her at all. You scuffled and she fell, hitting her head." I looked back at her. "And you thought she was dead."

Her eyes became enormous, boiling with a terrible new fear.

"She drowned, Ms. Goodwin. She was alive when you pushed her over the rail of the bridge."

Without warning her stomach betrayed her. I turned away as she fouled the Persian rug, gasping between retching spells. The stench stung my nose. When she regained control, she stood and rushed out of the room. I started to follow her, but I heard water running, a door slam, the lock click. I sat back down to wait.

The water stopped. I made a couple of notes in my notebook. A dog barked somewhere. And my head exploded.

*   *   *

When I came to, the house was quiet. I touched the back of my head and my hand came away red and sticky. I pushed myself up to my knees, fighting against blacking out again.

I looked at my watch, but I couldn't get my brain to calculate how much time had passed. When I was finally on my feet and confident that I wasn't going to go down like a tree in the forest, I got my gun in my hand and started slowly and quietly through the house. I got only as far as the kitchen, where a door led into the garage. I opened it cautiously. Her ivory Mercedes was gone.

Stupid! Idiot! Sexist! I leaned against the door jamb and berated myself. *If it had been a man, you never would have let him out of your sight.*

My mind cleared a little more and I tried to fathom how she could have gotten behind me. I suddenly wondered if Roger Clarke had figured out why I was interested in the cake. I ran out of the house and across the lawn that separated his house from Marsha's. I still had the gun in my hand when I rang the bell. I shoved it quickly into the holster, thinking that if he wasn't there, one of the kids would answer, and if he was there, I didn't really need it.

A groggy Roger Clarke answered the door in green pajamas. "What is it?" He looked alarmed.

I hesitated to tell him. When he saw the yellow crime scene ribbons all around Marsha's house in the morning, he would find out then. He would be upset, and rightfully so I supposed, if he found out that way. He had a right to know.

"Close the door," I said.

He stepped out onto the porch and pulled the door behind him.

"Marsha Goodwin may have killed Mary."

"What!"

"She fled and I don't have time right now to tell you more."

"Marsha?"

"Goodnight, Roger." I left, but he followed me across the yard.

"Why?"

"Tomorrow, Roger. I'll tell you everything tomorrow." I went back to the cruiser and, with Roger still hovering around me, called for assistance. I also got a BOLO out on the Mercedes. Two squad cars arrived quickly. One of the patrolmen looked at the back of my head and called for an ambulance.

I took the other officer back into the house with me. Roger tried to follow, but I stopped him, telling him he couldn't enter the house. The patrolman and I confirmed that the rest of the house was empty. We put crime scene tape across the pantry. I wanted it undisturbed until I could get Horkheimer to process it for Mary's prints.

Back at the entry I noticed the empty spot on the narrow table just inside the door. There had been a tall, bronze something there on my previous visit – a vase, no, a statue. I had the patrolman use his flashlight to search under all the furniture. Nothing.

The ambulance arrived and the paramedics wanted me to go with them but, other than a gigantic headache, I felt okay, so I refused. They put something on my head that instantly took my mind off the headache. When it quit burning, they stuck a bandage on my scalp, and after getting my assurance that I would stop by the emergency room and let a doctor look at me, they left.

We taped the house and one of the patrolmen was posted there for the remainder of the night. Roger finally went home and I drove myself to the emergency room. A young Pakistani doctor probed and prodded my sore head, gave me a couple of capsules for the headache, and told me that other than having an odd shape for a few days, it would be as good as it ever was. A nurse redressed the ruptured skin and released me.

It was almost four when I took the pills and fell into my own bed. I slept right through the alarm. At 8:30 the telephone rang persistently, finally piercing the fog. It sounded like a fire bell going off inside my head and I struggled across to the desk to lift the receiver and stop the ringing.

"Stick, is that you? …Stick?"

It took a moment for me to realize that someone was talking into my ear. "Wha…yeah, it's me."

"This is Wayne."

"Yeah, g'mornin' Wayne."

"Come on, Stick, wake up. They found Marsha Goodwin's car."

A cold shower would have been less effective; I was suddenly wide awake. "Where?"

"Parked on the Monroe side of the Card Sound Bridge."

Nausea. "Goddamn it!"

"She's the one after all?"

"Yeah, you won the pot, Wayne. Only I still don't have a bit of evidence. Listen, can you do me a couple of favors?"

"Sure."

"Get in touch with a Key Largo cop named Horace Graves. Tell him you're calling for me and this is about the floater in Card Sound. Tell him what you know and ask him to get a diver in the water up there as soon as he can."

"Horace Graves," Wayne repeated.

"Then send Horkheimer back out to Marsha's house. Did you bring in the canister or just the necklace?"

"Just the necklace."

"Okay. I want him to dust everything he can in that closet for Mary Clarke's prints, particularly that canister and any others around it. Mary was trying to borrow a cup of powdered sugar, if that helps him any."

"And she saw the necklace?"

"That's what I think. As soon as I can get dressed, I'm going down to the bridge."

Morning traffic was snarled, but I hardly noticed. A tall redhead in a white jumpsuit, without the mettle to face the realities of her life, was on my mind. She couldn't face giving up any of her pretty things, so she stole the necklace. She couldn't face discovery, so she used force on Mary Clarke, deadly force. And now she couldn't face what she had done. I wondered where it started, where her priorities had gotten out of line. I was sick with the reality of where it seemed to be ending.

Horace was there when I arrived. They were still waiting on the diver who had to come up from Tavernier. The Mercedes was parked in the grass where the abutment began. It was unlocked, the key still in the ignition. Her purse was on the floor behind the passenger's seat, the contents spilling out.

The diver showed up then and we all went to the water's edge.

"What the hell happened to your head, Stick?" Horace asked.

"I went to sleep at the controls." I nodded toward the bubbles surfacing from the diver below. "She pounded me with a bronze statue."

"So she could get away and commit suicide? Are you sure she's down there?"

The seeming lack of logic had not really occurred to me. Maybe she wasn't down there at all. Maybe she just wanted us to think that she jumped, that her body was carried away with the ebbing tide. While we're looking for her here, she's already on a plane to Houston or LA, no debts and no crimes. Maybe I should...

All such thoughts were swept away as her bright red hair caught the morning sun. The diver pushed her to the surface from below and came swimming toward shore on his back, holding her shoulders to his chest. When he grounded, he stood up and backed out of the shallow water, his big flippers smacking the water with each step. He laid her down gently on a little patch of sand on Horace's side of the bridge.

Her skin was already almost transparent. Water ran out of every opening in her jumpsuit, cutting little rivulets in the soft sand. Her hands were free, but her feet were bound loosely, and strands of the light cord trailed a foot or so back toward the water.

"She was tied to a block," the diver volunteered. "I had to cut her loose. I'll go back for the block."

I stood looking down at her, wondering for the ten-thousandth time since I had taken the oath how things can go this wrong. Horace climbed back up the embankment and came back with a blanket, which we spread over Marsha Anne Tucker Goodwin, deceased.

The diver resurfaced with the block and the rest of the cord that had fastened Marsha to it. The block looked the same to me as the one that Mary had been tied to. The cord was a little different, but similar. The way the two women had been attached to the blocks was not alike at all. Mary had been laced tightly to hers; Marsha's noosed ankles were connected with about a foot of cord, and the block tethered to that with an additional three feet of line.

"She could still walk and carry the block with that rig," Horace observed.

I could understand why Marsha would tie herself the way she did. But the haphazard way the cord was wrapped around her ankles and around the block made me indistinctly uneasy.

The Monroe medical examiner arrived, and they took her to Key Largo. The tow truck pulled up, but before they removed the car, I knew I wanted a look in the trunk. Horace and I went back up to the car and I slid behind the wheel to get the key.

"Nice car," Horace said, leaning in.

I squared myself in the seat, reclining against the supple leather. "Yes it is. What the...! Look at this."

"What?"

"I can barely reach the pedals the way this seat is adjusted."

"She was a tall woman, Stick."

"Not this tall." I had to slide down in the seat to get pressure on the brake.

"She tied the block on while she was still in the car," Horace suggested. "She had to move the seat back to do it."

I nodded. "Yeah, maybe. Did anyone see her drive up? A fisherman maybe?"

"We haven't really asked, but we will."

The seat position was gnawing at me. "Yeah, do that. I've already spoiled the keys, but get your guys to check the wheel for prints other than hers?"

"It's leather, Stick. Good luck with that."

"Shit."

The trunk was empty. There were little pebbles on the carpet that hid the spare tire. I picked a few up and looked at them
more closely. Loose aggregate, maybe from the block still sitting
down on the sand where only the rivulets evidenced her passing.
I ran my hand along the crevice at the rear of the trunk where the
floor joined the body panel. Near the right side I felt something.
I grasped it and brought it out into the bright sunlight.

It was the broken corner of a concrete block.

24

MONDAY

THE BROKEN PIECE WAS A PERFECT MATCH as the missing corner of the block that Mary Clarke had been tied to. A ball of cord from her kitchen was the same as the cord Mary had been tied with. Horkheimer found Mary Clarke's prints all over the canister that had hidden the stolen necklace. Maybe she had opened it. Or maybe she had accidentally knocked it over. We would never know.

Marsha's purse contained a safety deposit box key. Once opened with a court order, inside we found Mary's rings – the emerald one and the wedding set.

On Tuesday afternoon, the day of the week Marsha would have visited, I stopped by the only building supply close to her house and found a kid who remembered loading two concrete blocks into the back of a light-colored Mercedes for a very tall red-headed lady.

Horace Graves called to tell me that the only prints found anywhere on the car belonged to Marsha Goodwin. The Monroe medical examiner had determined that she was alive when she went into the water, had found no other pertinent evidence, and had officially ruled her death a suicide. He was sending me a copy of the death certificate. They had not found anyone who had seen her driving to the bridge.

I had driven out to Roberts & Wilson on Thursday to bring Roger Clarke up to date, a day later than I had promised. Carmen lacked her usual effervescence, and I guessed that things between her and Roger were not going well. I felt nominally sorry for her, more so for Adam and Cheri; I was sure that she would have been good with them.

I gave Roger the whole story. He seemed off and hardly reacted. It must have been a shock to him. He had seen Marsha as a – what was his word – lifesaver. She had taken over for Mary, had shown great compassion. To suddenly learn that this angel of mercy was the angel of death must have shorted his circuits. He already had Steiner's death on his conscience. This second error in judgment, no matter how justifiable, had to leave him wondering about everyone around him. As I left his office, I couldn't help wondering how all of this was going to affect him.

That afternoon, I finally stamped the file on Mary Frances Clarke CLOSED and laid it aside to await the death certificate before putting it away for good. Wayne came around in the afternoon, either to congratulate me on closing the case or to seek kudos for being almost right almost from the start. Both were accomplished.

"You don't seem very pleased to have this one in the bag," he observed.

A clear indication of my frame of mind, I winced at his choice of phrases. "I don't know. Mary's death was really an accident. Marsha never meant to kill her. I just can't feel good about the price she paid."

"Whoa, Stick. That was the lady's decision. You can't go

around beating yourself up for that one."

"Horace found it strange that she would scramble my brain with a hunk of bronze only to go immediately and throw herself off a bridge."

"Mmm. Many people would rather die than go to jail, or even be exposed. The jig was up and she knew it."

"Okay," I said. "But why off the bridge with a concrete block?"

Wayne shrugged. "Why not? An eye for an eye."

"Yeah, that's exactly what keeps going through my mind. But that's vengeance, Wayne, not repentance."

Wayne gave me a sidelong look. "This thing is hung in your craw, ain't it boy?"

"It is," I admitted.

"Truth is, it doesn't seem all that odd to me that if you found out you had killed someone in a particularly cruel way and you regretted it, you might want to pay for that in the same coin."

"Yeah, I know. And her seat was too far back for her to drive the car because she had moved it back to tie herself to the block. And the cord was different because she just grabbed a different ball from the drawer. And it wasn't neat like Mary's because she was tying herself, in the dark, frightened of being discovered, and knowing that she was about to die. And she got behind me by slipping out the back of the house and coming back in the front door. Individually, I can explain every one of them logically. Taken all together they give me a bad feeling."

Wayne put it all together. "Roger Clarke?"

"Yeah."

"But you told me he was still there after she was gone."

"He was."

"Hell, Stick, he didn't even know she was the one," Wayne added.

"I didn't think so."

"And now you do?"

"I don't know. Suppose he did. Suppose he figured out about the cake, realized that Mary must have left the house and gone over to Marsha's to borrow the missing sugar.

"After I leave, he walks over and sees my car in her drive. The windows in the living room are all open. He hears our exchange, slips in the still unlocked front door, beans me, and abducts a terrified Marsha Goodwin."

"But he was at home. He can't be on the way to the bridge and at home at the same time."

I raised my left hand. "He doesn't go to the bridge. He puts Marsha in the trunk of her own car, backs it out of her garage, drives around the corner and parks it in his garage. He leaves Marsha in the trunk and goes inside to put on his pajamas."

"Then he answers the door," Wayne interrupted, "cool as a well-digger's belt buckle, hangs around with you till 3:00 a.m., backs the Mercedes he knows is red-hot out of the garage with a patrolman on station next door, drives halfway across the county at an hour when every second car is one of us, does the deed, leaves the car but somehow gets back across the county before the kids wake up and miss him, showers, shaves, steps into his favorite blue Brooks Brothers, and goes into work to make another million." He finished with a flourish. "Sounds reasonable to me."

"You're right, I know. It's just that there is something about that guy that makes me look for a way for him to be involved. Hell, the Steiner thing may even have happened exactly like he says." I patted the thick file folder lying on the corner of the desk. "Marsha Goodwin couldn't live with what she had done so she elected to die symbolically, and that's it. This case is closed."

"There you go."

"Still, I wish I had taken a look in his garage."

"You're hopeless," Wayne said, lifting himself out of his chair and heading back to his own domain.

Whether I was pleased with the final resolution of the case or not, the lieutenant was. He was also aware of how many hours I had already put in for the week. For both reasons, I wasn't expected in the office for the remainder of the week.

I slept until noon on Friday, then in the afternoon picked up Helen Steiner and her new board and spent the rest of the afternoon showing her how to rig it and giving additional sailing lessons. It was evident that the student would soon surpass the teacher.

It was late Friday evening when I finally got an answer at Cristine's number. She told me she had arrived from London only minutes before I called and was headed for 12 hours of sleep. She invited me for brunch at 11:00 the following morning.

* * *

"I thought I had been such a leech that you decided to move away," I told her over fresh melon.

She laughed. "Patty is visiting her mom in Wisconsin, and this trip came up unexpectedly. I tried to call you every night, but you weren't home."

"Yeah, I was working late a lot." After I said it, it sounded like a very lame alibi to me, and I wondered what she thought

I was really doing.

"The case with the two little girls?" She thought I was work-ing. She would, of course. It all came back to me, how comfortable she made me feel.

"Uh-huh. Good melon. I taught one of them to sail." I told her about Helen Steiner.

"That's nice. How is the case going?"

"Solved." I tried to seem happy about it.

"Really?"

"Thanks to you."

"Right."

"No, really," I said. I told her how the borrowed spice, her familiarity with her neighbor's pantry, had given me the idea that Mrs. Clarke might have done the same thing.

"I've never been in Rosie's pantry. She has a rack on the kitchen wall with all her spices."

"You're kidding. Well, it doesn't matter. It made me realize that the reason I wasn't finding any clues was because no crime had occurred at Mrs. Clarke's. If I had been looking in the right place from the start, it might have ended differently."

We spent the rest of the day doing the things that new couples do: a walk in the nearby park, an afternoon matinee to escape the heat, a triple scoop of Häagen-Dazs, a dozen roses from a street vendor, a late dinner of seafood crepes at a tiny and dimly lit French restaurant.

Sunday morning, we shared the newspaper on the balcony as dozens of white sails peacefully zig-zagged across the jade bay. When I picked up the local-news section, Arturo Ribera's photograph was featured prominently on the front page. Wanda's story was there, all right, but only as a lead-in to a more complete report on Ribera. The *Herald* must have already been on the scent when I called; my columnist friend shared the byline with two other staff reporters.

It was a character assassination – no, make that annihilation. If Ribera's legitimate partners were not already in too deep, they would damn sure bail out now. The attorneys down at the *Herald* would be busy for a while. I wondered what danger the reporters might be in.

Monday arrived too quickly, with memories of Sunday running through my head like a movie shot through a soft lens. I was still smiling at mid-morning when Horace Graves called to get additional information on Marsha Goodwin to close his case. I filled in all his blanks.

"One other thing, Stick. We did find a fisherman that says he saw a man on the bridge about 4:30. He didn't see the car. I thought it might have been her, as tall as she was, but this guy says no. The person he saw was a man, but it was too dark to see his face. What do you think?"

A cold, liquid darkness enveloped me. I felt the weight of Cheri Clarke pulling me under.

"Doesn't sound like much to go on," I heard myself saying.

"Yeah, that's what I think, too." He moved on. "Did I tell you I bought a new boat? Come on down next weekend and we'll go after the big one."

"Maybe I will, FB," I said. "Maybe I will."

For decades Don Casey has been North America's most consulted authority on the outfitting and care of sailboats. He has previously published ten books that include both the acclaimed *Don Casey's Complete Illustrated Sailboat Maintenance Manual* and *This Old Boat,* widely considered a classic in the genre. Don's clear and entertaining writing has helped generations of owners solve their boat problems.

He has now turned his hand to a different sort of problem solving: *Marjoram & Mace* is his first mystery novel.

Don lives in Miami, Florida with his wife, Olga.